TENKO REUNION

The BBC TV Production of TENKO REUNION

Marion Jefferson	ANN BELL
Dr Beatrice Mason	STEPHANIE COLE
Sister Ulrica	PATRICIA LAWRENCE
Mrs Forster-Brown	ELIZABETH CHAMBERS
Dorothy Bennett	VERONICA ROBERTS
Kate Norris	CLAIRE OBERMAN
Jake Haulter	DAMIEN THOMAS
Christina Campbell	EMILY BOLTON
Maggie Carter	ELIZABETH MICKERY
Alice Courtenay	CINDY SHELLEY
Stephen Wentworth	PRESTON LOCKWOOD
Teddy Forster-Brown	ROBERT LANG
Duncan Fraser	CHRISTIAN RODSKA
Lau Peng	SWEE HOE LIM
Mr Courtenay	BERNARD GALLAGHER

Produced by	KEN RIDDINGTON
Directed by	MICHAEL OWEN MORRIS
Script editor	DEVORA POPE

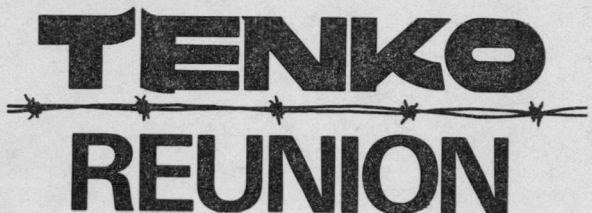

TENKO REUNION

A novel by
Anne Valery

based on the screenplay by
Jill Hyem

CORONET BOOKS
Hodder and Stoughton

Based on the series created by
Lavinia Warner

© Prime Productions Ltd 1986

Coronet edition 1985

British Library C.I.P.

Valery, Anne
Tenko reunion.
I. Title
823'.914[F]   PR6072.A/

ISBN 0-340-39111-1

Printed and bound in Great Britain for
Hodder and Stoughton Paperbacks, a
division of Hodder and Stoughton Ltd.,
Mill Road, Dunton Green, Sevenoaks,
Kent (Editorial Office: 47 Bedford
Square, London, WC1 3DP) by
Richard Clay (The Chaucer Press) Ltd.,
Bungay, Suffolk. Photoset by
Rowland Phototypesetting Ltd.,
Bury St Edmunds, Suffolk.

To 'Ted' F. L. Russell, who was there.

Biographies

Marion Jefferson

Born: 1904, in Ascot, Berkshire.
Father: Lt Colonel Peter 'Teddy' Lisle. Died in action in the First World War.
Mother: amateur musician, who suffered from chronic ill health. died, 1949.
Education: Roedean, Sussex, and The Princess Louise Finishing School for Girls, Montreux, Switzerland.

Soon after leaving her finishing school and 'coming out', Marion met and married Clifford Jefferson, an officer in her father's regiment. Both families considered the match very suitable, and the couple settled in Aldershot where Clifford was stationed.

In 1929, after an earlier miscarriage, Marion gave birth to their only child, Ben. She was a devoted mother, who was broken-hearted when, at the age of seven, Ben was sent away to prep school prior to going to his father's old school, Wellington – a school much favoured by the military.

In 1937, Clifford was posted to the North-West Frontier of India; and after various other postings and the outbreak of the Second World War, to Singapore. Here, Clifford was one of the few Staff Officers who believed that the Japanese might invade by land from the north, rather than by sea.

Up until the Japanese invasion, Marion had led the life of a typical army officer's wife: entertaining her husband's fellow officers and their wives; sitting on various committees, and helping with entertainments for other ranks. Increasingly, however, she felt that her life lacked a centre, especially after being posted abroad which meant that Ben could only visit his parents during the long summer holidays. It was not until British refugees arrived in Singapore after fleeing from the advancing enemy that Marion was able to seek fulfilment outside her family, helping to organise the resettlement of the refugees.

Because of her work she refused an early evacuation, finally leaving on one of the last ships to get away. The ship was torpedoed by the Japanese, and she – together with Doctor Mason, Nurse Kate Norris, Dorothy Bennett and her baby, and Christina Campbell – were interned in a camp on one of the islands.

From 1942 – 1945, Marion was interned in three camps. Throughout this period, she was the leader of the British women, and this brought her into contact with the camp commandant, Yamauchi.

The war in the Far East ended in the summer of 1945, when the Allies dropped two atomic bombs on Japan. After Marion's camp was liberated, the women were sent to Singapore to recover, prior to being shipped home. It was here that Marion was reunited with Clifford, who had spent much of the war in England. Initially very happy, Marion started to drink when her newly acquired independence of mind threatened the marriage. However, the couple managed to patch over the cracks, and in October Marion left for Britain, and was reunited with her son, Ben, now almost grown-up.

Clifford and Marion settled in Primrose Hill, London, though their marriage was still fraught with problems, and they were subsequently divorced.

Up to her internment, Marion's life had been typical of many middle-class girls of the period. A dutiful daughter who nursed her mother and deferred to her father's wishes not to marry too young; an army officer's wife who did all that she could to help her husband's career; and a devoted mother, who nevertheless accepted that her son had to be sent away to school. It was this in particular that sowed the seeds of discontent, though

Marion did not break out of the mould until the Japanese invasion.

More than any of the other women, Marion found fulfilment in the camps, for she thrived in her position of responsibility, in making her own decisions, and in discovering that women could be as resourceful and as strong in their purpose as men.

Doctor Beatrice Mason

Born: 1897, in Skipton, Yorkshire. The elder of two daughters.
Father: Vicar of the Church of England.
Education: local school, scholarship to a grammar school, medical school in Edinburgh.

In 1901, the Reverend Mason was transferred to a slum parish in Leeds, and it was here that Beatrice grew up. Hating the squalor of the district where she lived, Beatrice was the odd one out in the family. While her sister was content to stay at home and marry young, she was determined to become a doctor.

After completing her training, Beatrice specialised in tropical diseases and in 1934 obtained a post in the hospital in Kuala Lumpur. In 1939, she transferred to the Alexander Hospital in Singapore, and it was here that she met Kate Norris who was one of her nurses.

Because of her early life in the slums, Beatrice was almost fanatical about order, hygiene, and treatment 'by the book'; this attitude, which was a protection against doubt, distanced her from her colleagues, who respected rather than liked her. To compensate for her loneliness, Beatrice's career became her life, until in 1942 she was interned in the same camp as Marion.

Confronted by the unspeakable conditions and scant medicine, Beatrice's attitude to patients and their treatment altered radically, for she grew to recognise the importance of human contact and sympathy. Often, it was these qualities alone that pulled a patient back from the grave. However, once she had allowed her emotions to encroach on her nursing, they spilled over into all her contacts, and she began to express feelings and doubts that she had never voiced before – especially to Nurse Nellie Keene, with whom she had worked in Singapore.

When Nellie was sent to another camp, Beatrice leant more and more on Kate Norris for, with her eyesight failing, there were many treatments that she could no longer perform alone.

On the women's transfer to a second camp, Beatrice was forced to work under Doctor Trier, a French woman. From the start Beatrice hated her, for Trier was even more distant than she had once been – indeed her only concern seemed to be the writing of a secret report on the effects of malnutrition. However, when Doctor Trier was repatriated to Vichy France, Beatrice promised to continue the notes, and this she did until the day of liberation.

Once in Singapore, Beatrice was convinced that with spectacles she would be able to see as well as ever. However, later she learnt that she would gradually lose her sight. Depressed that she might have to return to her family when she could no longer see, Beatrice was given the chance of working in a centre for the natives of Singapore, which was started by an ex-Changi prisoner, Stephen Wentworth, and ably assisted by Joss, a close friend from the camps.

Joss's death forced Beatrice to come to a decision, for in her Will she stipulated that she would leave £52,000 to the Centre, on condition that Beatrice and Stephen run it.

Although a kindly and perceptive doctor and friend, Beatrice can be difficult, for she flares at the slightest injustice – a temper born from the injustices meted out by her father.

Sister Ulrica

Born: 1886, in Antwerp, Holland. The youngest child with two brothers.

Father: a general, and the son of a long line of distinguished public servants.

Mother: a rich aristocrat, whose dowry included a large house in the country.

Education: governess and tutors.

Ulrica grew up with the belief that having been given so much she should repay it through service to the community. Encouraged by her old governess, in 1908 Ulrica was accepted into the Catholic Church as a novice. Her family strongly disapproved.

In 1919, Sister Ulrica worked in the administration office of her Order and in 1922 was sent to teach in a convent school in the Dutch East Indies. From there she was transferred to the St Teresa orphanage. A year later, in 1938, she was promoted to Sister Consultor, the head of administration.

Due to the chaos caused by the Japanese invasion early in 1942, Ulrica did not receive the monthly orphanage funds from Singapore. Alone, she travelled to the city and was trapped there, offering her services to the Alexander Hospital, where she met Marion Jefferson, Nurse Kate Norris and Doctor Mason. Evacuated from Singapore just before it fell, Ulrica was sent to a convent on one of the islands, and it was here that she was captured. Together with Dominica Van Meyer and other Dutch women and nuns, Ulrica was interned in the same camp as Marion and her friends, where she was the leader of the Dutch.

However, the relationship between the British and the Dutch was not a happy one: the Dutch, having travelled overland, were able to bring many luxuries with them, whereas the British had nothing, and for the first six months worked for the Dutch. Added to this, the Dutch considered that the British were trouble-makers, especially after the failed escape of two British internees. Always a woman to obey the rules, Ulrica was horrified by the British action. Strangely, it was this very action that brought the two nationalities together, for they worked side by side for the release of the two internees who were locked in the punishment hut by night, and tied to stakes during the day.

Ultimately Ulrica and the British became very close, for, separated from other nuns and deprived of her habit, she learnt to see life through the eyes of the lay women. No longer under the Church, she began to query many of the rules of her calling. Indeed, she attended a suicide's funeral and stood by Dorothy Bennett during her abortion – an act she abhorred. Because of her new-found independence of thought, a visiting priest persuaded Ulrica to transfer to a convent internment camp, where she would again be under the discipline of the Church.

After her release in 1945, Sister Ulrica was sent to convalesce in a convent in Singapore, and it was here that she was reunited with her friends from camp. Again Ulrica's doubts surfaced, and though she remained a nur, she was allowed to leave her Order and work in a leper colony up-country.

Dorothy Bennett

Born: 1913, in Edgware, London.
Father: a solicitor's clerk.
Mother: a shop assistant until her marriage.
Education: local school, followed by one year in a private school.

When Dorothy left school in 1929, she wanted to be a secretary. However her parents – especially her dominant mother – would not allow it. Deeply conservative and 'respectable', they believed that a daughter should stay at home until she married. Ever the dutiful daughter, Dorothy, complied with their wishes.

In 1934, the boy-next-door, Dennis, returned home on leave from his job in Robinson's Department Store in Singapore. At their first meeting, Dennis fell in love with Dorothy who, if she did not return the love in the same measure, saw marriage as an escape from home.

In 1936, Dorothy and Dennis were married in the local Methodist Church, and set sail for Singapore and Dennis' bungalow on the outskirts. It was here that Dorothy settled down to be a good suburban housewife – everything that her parents and husband would wish.

Early in 1942, a baby daughter, Violet, was born. Because the baby was only a month old when the Japanese invaded Malaya, the family stayed on in Singapore until the very last moment. When they were captured, Dennis assured Dorothy if they did everything that the Japanese asked of them, they would be unharmed. Dennis was shot.

With Marion and the other women, Dorothy arrived at the first camp in a state of shock, which was not helped when Violet developed dysentery. Terrified, Dorothy worked for a Dutch internee, Mrs Van Meyer, in order to earn money to buy food for her sick child. Despite the extra rations, Violet died.

The double shock of the death of both her daughter and her husband stirred Dorothy from her lifelong passivity, and her true nature emerged: that of a tough and determined survivor. In order to get food and cigarettes for herself, Dorothy began to sleep with the Japanese guards, and indeed, together with Blanche Simmons, became one of the camp tarts. Despite this, her closest friend was Sister Ulrica, for they both possessed that rare quality: honesty.

In the second camp Dorothy became pregnant by a Japanese guard and, despite Sister Ulrica's pleadings, had an abortion. Afterwards, Dorothy became very ill, and it was Sister Ulrica's devotion that helped to save her life. When her closest friend was transferred to a convent camp, Dorothy was devastated.

In 1945, while recovering in Singapore, Dorothy was recognised by an internee from the second camp who reported to the R.A.P.W.I. officer, Phyllis Barlow, that Dorothy had been a tart and therefore a collaborator. In order to avert a scandal, Dorothy was flown back to London.

Here, Dorothy put her knowledge of antiques – acquired from Jake Haulter, a friend in Singapore – to good use. She opened a junk shop which prospered and in 1949 moved to a shop in Church Street, Kensington.

Despite her honesty, Dorothy remains an enigma, for her reaction to any person or situation is unpredictable.

Nurse Kate Norris

Born: 1916, in Australia.
Father: owned a garage and small farm in the outback.
Mother: a New Zealander who helped on the farm.
Education: local school.

In 1930, because of her mother's illness, Kate was forced to leave school and help on the farm. Despite this, she managed to complete her education, and became a student nurse.

Initially, Kate was not a dedicated nurse, and only became one in order to travel. To this end, once her training was completed, she sailed for Singapore and her first post at the Alexander Hospital.

In 1940, after only two weeks at the hospital, Kate was transferred to the surgical ward under Doctor Beatrice Mason. It was not a happy working relationship, for Doctor Mason was a pedant, while Kate was too independent and free with her opinions.

During the Japanese bombardment of Singapore, Kate became engaged to Tom, a young Englishman. They escaped from Singapore on the same ship as Marion. After being taken prisoner, Tom was sent to the men's camp, possibly the same one as Jan Van Meyer.

During the next few years of internment Kate grew up, changing from a hearty extrovert to a serious-minded and devoted nurse. Even her relationship with Doctor Mason changed, for in the end they came to respect and like each other. Not that there weren't occasional clashes – deeply religious, Kate was horrified at Beatrice helping with Dorothy's abortion.

In 1945, when Kate arrived in Singapore, she discovered that Tom was alive, though very ill with tuberculosis. A few weeks later Tom died.

When Kate sailed home for Australia, she had made up her mind that she would follow in Beatrice's footsteps and become a doctor.

Dominica Van Meyer

Born: Holland.
Father: private means.
(Note: Dominica is most elusive about her early life, especially her date of birth. All that is known, is that she had two sisters and was educated privately.)

At the age of seventeen, Dominica married Jan Van Meyer, a businessman and the son of a distinguished family. In 1927, because of a scandal involving Jan, the Van Meyers moved to a family estate in the Dutch East Indies. Here Dominica entertained lavishly, for she saw herself as a leader of the Dutch social set. In 1942, the Van Meyers were taken prisoner by the Japanese, and Dominica and Sister Ulrica joined Marion and her friends in camp. Dominica's husband was sent to a men's camp nearby.

Because Dominica already lived on the island, she was able to bring many luxuries into the camp, and, though grumbling more than anyone, for the first few months scarcely suffered. Always a hypochondriac, Dominica was convinced that she would die once her money was spent. She proved to be one of nature's survivors however, and despite bouts of beri-beri, came through without suffering any lasting damage.

When the women moved to the second camp, Dominica became convinced that her husband must be dead, for he was not on the Japanese list of next-of-kin. After her release, however, she discovered that Jan was very much alive. Far from being pleased, she was deeply upset. The marriage had never been a happy one, and she had fallen in love with a stuffy English major. Despite this, she decided to return to her husband, for she had no money of her own and she dreaded the thought of being poor.

Though a selfish, snobbish and vain woman, Dominica was ultimately accepted by the other internees – perhaps because she made them laugh, and in her odd moments of courage, when they saw that beneath all the boasting she was a lonely and insecure woman.

Maggie Carter (née Thorpe)

Born: 1918, in Sheffield, Yorkshire.
Father: steel worker. Committed suicide in 1932.
Mother: washerwoman. Died of tuberculosis in 1930.
Education: local schools. For the last two years of schooling, Maggie seldom attended, for she had to look after her father and her three sisters and two brothers. She left school in 1931.

After the authorities discovered that Maggie was pregnant by her father, the father was sent to prison where he killed himself, and her sisters and brothers were boarded out. The shock of what had happened caused Maggie to miscarry, and at the age of fourteen she went to work in a mill.

In 1937, Maggie and a friend set sail for Shanghai, where they had been promised a job in a bar. They worked their passage by cleaning the cabins of the crew. In 1940, Maggie moved to a bar in Singapore, and then to a nightclub, where she worked as a cigarette girl.

In 1942, Maggie was interned; two and a half years later, she joined Marion and her friends in the third camp. Here, she became very friendly with Blanche Simmons who later died. After the liberation in 1945, and while the women were waiting in camp to be flown to Singapore, Maggie slept with an ex-P.O.W. She never knew his name. Convalescing in Singapore, Maggie met Jake Haulter, with whom she had an affair. When she discovered that she was pregnant by the P.O.W., Jake offered to arrange an abortion, but Maggie decided to have the baby. A good friend of Dorothy Bennett's – partly because they had both been camp tarts – on her return to London, she moved in with Dorothy and helped in her junk shop.

In 1946, a daughter, Blanche, was born and in 1947, Maggie married a railway worker and shop steward, Jim Carter. They moved to a rented house in the East End of London and it was here that a son was born in 1950.

Despite many tragedies, Maggie is a resilient woman, and is now happily married and devoted to her two children. Partly because of her husband's job as a shop steward, she has become a fanatical socialist and hates any form of class injustice.

Christina Campbell

Born: 1920, in Singapore.
Father: a Scottish school teacher.
Mother: Chinese. Both parents died before Christina was interned.
Education: local school, and by her father. She has a natural gift for languages and speaks five.

Born and bred in Singapore, Christina soon learned that it was best for a half-caste to be subservient and eager to please. She was very aware of the many places from which she was barred because of her colour.

In 1940, Christina became a guide for various groups of tourists, and it was then that she met Simon, a British Army lieutenant. It was love at first sight, and it was Simon who helped Christina leave Singapore on the same ship as Marion. Before the couple separated, Simon gave Christina a ring and promised to wait for her.

During her time in the first camp, Christina learnt some Japanese, and it was because of this talent for languages that she worked for Commandant Yamauchi in the camp's office. Here, she stole paper for Marion's diary and the camp's newspaper. Many of the internees were jealous of Christina because she had a 'clean' job and did not have to do the heavier work. When Rose, an internee, was betrayed and shot, many of the women accused Christina of the crime. Although it was later discovered that a friend of Marion's, Lillian, had betrayed Rose, Christina never forgot the injustice of the accusation.

On liberation, Christina planned to join her grandmother in Scotland, but she changed her mind and remained in Singapore – partly because she had discovered that Simon had married an English nurse. Finally able to accept that she was half Chinese and had been born and bred in the Far East, Christina decided to help at the Centre for the native refugees. Christina now teaches at the new Centre, a strong and confident woman.

Alice Courtenay

Born: 1929, in Mayfair, London.
Father: Director of various companies, including a mining company in Shanghai.
Education: governess, followed by private schools.

In 1939, Alice and her parents visited Mr Courtenay's company in Shanghai and when her father returned to England, Alice and her mother stayed on for a few months.

At the outbreak of war in Europe, Mr Courtenay suggested that his family remain in the East, because he believed that London and the major cities would be heavily bombed. In the spring of 1940, when Alice and her mother were about to return home, Mrs Courtenay contracted rheumatic fever. In 1941, Alice and her mother moved to Singapore prior to returning to England. Unfortunately Alice caught pneumonia, and their return was once again delayed. Trapped by the advance of the Japanese, they were taken prisoner in Singapore, and shipped to an island camp.

In 1942, Alice and her mother transferred to a second camp, where they met Maggie Thorpe. Due to an outbreak of cholera, the camp was closed, and the three women were transferred to the third camp, where they joined Marion and her friends.

Early in 1945 Mrs Courtenay died. Because of her loneliness, Alice became very close to Maggie while looking to Marion for motherly guidance.

While recovering in Singapore, the child-like Alice was deeply disturbed when a young man tried to make advances. Already traumatised by the camps and the death of her mother, this small incident reinforced Alice's terror of the unknown; although she appeared to recover, she was beset with fears which she couldn't voice to anyone, especially her father when she was reunited with him in London.

Stephen Wentworth

Born: 1875, in Woodham Ferrers, Essex.
Father: an historian, specialising in eighteenth-century London.
Mother: author of children's books. Both parents were Fabians.
Education: tutors, followed by Oxford. A degree in English Literature.

Having been left some money by his godmother, Stephen moved to Paris after University; in 1901, when his money ran out, he became the representative of a British publishing house. In 1911, he transferred to the publisher's London office, volunteering for the army at the outbreak of the First World War.

In 1918, Stephen was wounded in France and returned to his parents' house, where he lived until 1921 when his parents were killed in a train crash. Unemployed and now broke, Stephen took a post in a prep school. He disliked the job, for he was very poorly paid and did not take kindly to a fixed timetable. Fortunately, in 1929, he inherited five hundred pounds and a house in Shanghai. He immediately set sail for the Far East, determined to write the definitive English novel. It was to be called 'The Fall From Grace'.

In 1936, and by now into the fifth draft of the novel, Stephen met Monica Radcliffe and was bullied into teaching at her school for the waifs and strays of Shanghai. In 1941, though he adored Monica, he accepted the headmastership of a native school in Singapore. The novel was now into its tenth draft.

In 1942, Stephen was captured and interned in Changi jail. On his release from camp at the end of the war, Stephen returned to his school only to find it full of ex-pupils and their parents who had nowhere to live. He did the best he could for them.

Desperate to find out what had happened to his old friend Monica, Stephen visited Raffles Hotel, hoping that one of the ex-internees might know. Here he met Joss Holbrook, and learnt that Monica had died in a camp.

Stephen took to Joss immediately, and persuaded her to help him at his centre for refugees. After her death, Beatrice replaced Joss at the Centre, which has now moved into larger premises.

Jake Haulter

Born: 1904, in Shanghai.
Father: minor Swiss Diplomat with business interests in the Far East, son of a French Swiss father and an English mother.
Mother: Indian.
Education: prep school and Marlborough, from which he was expelled.

In the aftermath of the First World War, Jake drifted to Paris where he married a rich American alcoholic. Divorced in 1927 and for the first time forced to earn a living, he joined the P. & O. shipping line as an Entertainments Officer, but jumped ship in Singapore. Such was his charm that he managed to be re-employed in the local P. & O. office, and was soon promoted.

By 1939, Jake had become an expert in transportation, specialising in tours up country for cruise passengers. On the side, as the sole Far East representative, he sold American cars. At the outbreak of war, Jake's job became a Reserved Occupation, and he helped to co-ordinate the movement of supplies from the Singapore docks. Throughout the war, he remained in the city, for he held a Swiss passport and was therefore a neutral. While working as a go-between for the Japanese and the embassies, he managed to smuggle news of the war to the natives and the staff of Raffles Hotel – all gleaned from the banned B.B.C. broadcasts.

Always a fly operator, when peace was declared Jake turned to wheeling and dealing on the black market.

Although he was never caught, the Establishment treated him with reserve. Because of his reputation and his colour, he had no close friends in Singapore society. While the ex-internees were resting in Raffles Hotel, Jake became particularly friendly with Maggie Thorpe and Dorothy Bennett. It was he who introduced Dorothy to the possibility of making a living from antiques. Although more interested in Dorothy, he had a brief affair with Maggie and, despite suggesting an abortion, was a great comfort to her when she decided to have her baby.

Jake now has a thriving car-hire firm, and other more dubious sidelines that he will not discuss.

Some of Those Who Have Died

Blanche Simmons

Once a hostess in a nightclub, Blanche was one of Marion's group in the three camps. She was particularly friendly with Dorothy Bennett and Maggie Carter, partly because she too earned money as a camp tart. She died in a prison cell in the third camp. Blanche was a brave and humorous Cockney, who hated the class system.

Nurse Nellie Keene

Before the war, Nellie worked under Doctor Mason in Singapore, and became a close friend in the first camp. Subsequently, she was sent to a separate camp, and, worn out by nursing, died just before liberation.

Susie

Died at the age of eleven. She was particularly close to Doctor Mason.

The Lady Jocelyn Holbrook – 'Joss'

Born: 1873, the only daughter of Viscount Ashwood.
Married: Bunny Fitzroy, an actor, in 1919. Divorced in
  1926.

From an early age, Joss refused to conform or to be a
debutante. Instead, she went up to Cambridge to study,
although women could not take degrees.* It was there
that she met her great friend Monica Radcliffe. Over the
years, the friends were suffragettes, ambulance drivers
in the First World War; and afterwards were caught up in
many causes that championed the underdog. In the
1930s, Monica went to teach in Shanghai, where Joss
joined her a few years later.

When the friends were taken prisoner by the Japanese,
they were separated. Monica died in a camp soon afterwards.

In 1945, while in Singapore waiting to go home, Joss
met Stephen Wentworth. Together they ran an unofficial
centre for native refugees. However, in October, after
being attacked by a thief, Joss died. She left £52,000 for a
new Centre, on condition that Doctor Mason and Stephen
Wentworth run it. Joss was a tough and much loved
woman, an example to all who knew her.

* Cambridge did not award degrees to women until the
late 1940s, long after Oxford.

Yamauchi, the Japanese Commandant

Born in 1887, into a Samurai family, distinguished by
generations of military excellence.

It was Yamauchi's ill health that demoted him to the
ignominious position of running a prison camp. Even to
be associated with prisoners – especially women – was a
shameful loss of face.

Yamauchi ran the camps strictly by the book, but on
occasion he showed compassion to many of the prison-

ers. However, he knew of the cruelties that took place though he distanced himself, literally, by turning his back, or absenting himself from interrogations. He was a man who, while disapproving of what he did, nevertheless did it because it was an order.

In 1945, Yamauchi was imprisoned in Changi jail, and soon afterwards was tried and hanged. It was the luck of the draw, as it always is in the aftermath of war, for many guiltier war criminals served prison sentences and subsequently went free.

Note: *R.A.P.W.I*: Recovery of Allied Prisoners of War and Internees.

1

London

Dearest Bea,

At long last a letter from you! You're almost as bad as Ben, but goodness what a joy when it *did* arrive.

I must say your new Centre sounds like a palace compared to that old one. My congratulations! Also to Stephen – despite what you say about him – and anyway he must be well into his seventies by now, so have a heart! Personally, I'd be completely daunted by your many projects, though Christina must be a real godsend. Not that she sounds at all like the shy Christina *I* knew, but then I suppose we've all changed in the past five years, though from the description of your running battle with the Sewage Department, you still sound exactly like the old Bea I knew and loved. In fact, I don't fancy the authorities' chances one bit, not when it comes to 'The Battle of the Drains'. More power to your elbow!

Incidentally, who is this Lau Peng? You keep on mentioning him doing this and that at the Centre, and how sterling he is, so when did *he* arrive?

Sitting here in my much too orderly drawing room

– too quiet by half now that Ben is up at Oxford – I feel such an overwhelming longing to be back in the East and especially Singapore: all that bustle and noise and muddle. (Odd how the memory of places seems to last so much longer than what happened in them – just as well, considering!)

Remember how the bustle hit us when we got off the plane in Singapore after the liberation? I often think what sights we must have looked in those rags and with sores all over us, but oh, *how happy* we were! I can still see you clutching your sacred First Aid box, specs askew, as you scurried after the stretchers in case the Red Cross hadn't *quite* understood what was wrong with *your* patients. Them were the days, as they say.

Which brings me to THE PLAN. Yesterday I was shopping in Kensington High Street – now almost cleared of bomb damage, thank goodness – and guess who I ran into? None other than our Dorothy, who's now so fashionably dressed that she made me feel most dreadfully frumpy and middle-aged. Anyway, she now has a very exclusive antique shop in Church Street, and is so busy she only just managed to squeeze me in for a tea at Derry & Tom's between her appointments, and that's when we cooked up THE PLAN. Remember how Kate suggested we should all have a reunion in exactly five years from the day we split up? Well, the five years will be up this October, so I took the bull by the horns and wrote straight off to Maggie, little Alice, Metro Goldwyn care of her bank in Singapore and Sister Ulrica at her last address up-country, *to suggest we do just that*! So now I enclose a note to Christina, and also a letter to Kate, as I seem to remember your mentioning that she's moved to a medical school in Sydney, and as her mentor I was sure you'd have her address.

So Bea, do say that despite your horrendous load of work, you'll find time for our reunion party in Raffles, and even a few lunches with your old friend.

I long for one of our 'Cosies' like we had in Camp – only this time we'll be able to indulge ourselves in a good meal and even a bottle of wine!

I enclose two pounds for flowers for Joss's grave – hope you can change them into Singapore dollars. I thought perhaps a bunch of those tiny orchids she was so fond of.

Write to me soon, dear Bea, and let me know how you feel about the reunion – personally I can't wait.

With much love, and give Stephen a hug from me.

Love,
Marion

P.S. Isn't it dreadful about these North Koreans invading the South? You'd think everyone would have had enough of war by now.

P.P.S. Still no news about where Blanche is buried, let alone any of the others. I'm afraid that the Powers-that-be just don't want to know, in fact, I get a distinct impression that our very existence is an embarrassment. However, I'll keep on keeping on.

Bennett Antiques,
Church Street,
Kensington

28th July, 1950

Dear Marion,

Tried to ring you all yesterday, but you were out.

Went to see Maggie as promised, and I *think* I've managed to persuade her to come out East, but it wasn't easy.

Poor love, she's living in a dreadful little house in the East End, and flat broke as per usual – but what can you expect with two kids and Jim on the railways! Anyway, I told her that if she didn't let me stump up for the trip the tax man would get it, and despite her strong Socialist principles (she's sounding more and more like Joss, only worse) she finally gave in. I must say she looks worn out, what with still feeding little Harry, and Blanche – all of four and a half would you believe – at that maddening stage of asking 'why' every two seconds. She's certainly a chip off the old block, if you can say that of a namesake. Remember, how Blanche used to go on and on about whatever bee she had in her bonnet?

While I remember, for God's sake don't mention politics when you do see Maggie, especially trade unions, or she'll bore you to death with the way the Conservatives and the Bank of England have undermined the Great Socialist Experiment. Also watch out you don't mention your old school as she thinks all public schools should have been scrapped. Not that I don't in principle, but then as far as I'm concerned principles are only for those who can afford them!

As I have a new and so far very efficient secretary, I suggest I get her to find out about our air flights, and if they do special rates for a three-week break, etc.?

Incidentally, you mentioned that your ex. and his wife are now in Rhodesia somewhere, and that the divorce was friendly, so I was wondering if you could contact him for me? What I want is the address of a trader, only I hear there's some good ivory knocking about – I'd pay the freight and any expenses of course, as long as the price is right! Because of the size of my shop, what I'm looking for are fairly small pieces for the Christmas trade. Thank God that at last people are starting to spend some money on luxuries – and about time too after five years of so-called peace!

Must rush as I'm off to a country auction in Suffolk, and my car's up the spout so I'll have to go by train, worse luck.

Love,
Dorothy

P.S. Have just had a word with my accountant, and he's confirmed that as I'll be buying for the shop I can charge my trip to expenses! So why don't you pretend you're writing a book about Life Behind the Wire, and see if you can swing it as well? No harm in trying!

The Sungei Kuching Estate,
Johore,
Malaya

18th August, 1950

Dearest Marion,

How very good it was to hear from my dear old friend, but *how* it upset me to hear you are divorced, when you both seemed so *very* right for each other. A younger woman I suppose, but then this generation does not have *our* moral standards, and certainly not our sense of what is *not* done. As for Van Meyer, I can only say that as a *collaborator* of those evil Japs, his death was God's judgement on him, just as my dear husband Teddy is God's reward for all the terrible suffering I went through. Only the other day I felt a sudden weakness of the limbs, for I am sure that one never quite recovers from the beriberi. But please, when you meet dear Teddy, do *not* say a word for he does so worry about me, and I try not to burden him with my little troubles. (Are you not impressed by my English, but then I too am now British and have a passport to prove it!)

The reunion is a truly wonderful idea, and it has quite raised my spirits in these terrible times. Not that I am not happy on our plantation, but it is not all a bed of roses as you English say, even though our bungalow is so very comfortable, and the servants simply *adore* me. It is this Emergency and these evil Communist terrorists that quite spoil everything.

When I think how good we have been to *all* the natives, I can only say it is most ungrateful that some want independence before the Government says they are ready. As for the bombs and shootings! How they can call themselves liberators of the country I do not know – they are just common murderers and should be hung or worse. (It is a war of, course, but they can't call it a war as it would affect insurance claims, especially the plantations, which have no soldiers to guard them though we pay more than enough in taxes!!)

I must confess that when I do manage to sleep – as you know, I have always been a martyr to insomnia – I have the most dreadful nightmares that dear Teddy has gone off to inspect the plantation and is carried back on a stretcher covered in blood. But then, it had always been the lot of us women, to wait and to weep for the ones we love!

Later. Dear Teddy had just come in from work, and insists that I take off a few days and stay with you all at Raffles! No thought for himself and *his* comfort! I will telephone and book tomorrow morning, so as to make quite sure we have rooms next to each other and then we can have long long talks together. I have always felt that we have so much more in common than the others, but then breeding tells. As to clothes, I shall only bring my most simple gowns, as I hear Maggie is most dreadfully poor and won't have our wardrobes.

How is your life? Are you still working for the Red Cross Library? Personally I would not have the stomach for it – all those sick people – so depressing. Also it would remind me of that *most* unsympathetic Mrs Bristow of R.A.P.W.I. When I think how she was supposed to look after us poor ex-prisoners and all she ever did was push us from room to room, and me a senior member of the group as far away from the bathroom as it was possible to put me. No wonder her husband died on her.

Looking forward so much to seeing you and exchanging all our news.

     With love to my dear friend,
     Dominica. (Metro Goldwyn!)

P.S. I enclose a photo of Teddy and me at the Tennis Club Dance in K.L. As you see I am not so slim as I once was, but as Teddy always says – a happy wife is pleasingly plump, and thank God I have kept the lines off my face. I do hate a woman who lets herself go.
P.P.S. I hear Stephen Wentworth is very old, and not much help with the Centre. Also, that Beatrice's eyes are worse, but then after what we have suffered, it's a miracle that we're alive at all!

     Primrose Hill,
     London NW3

     29th August, 1950

Dearest Bea,
     Congratulations on the drains!
   So thrilled that you're as keen as I am on the reunion. I can't wait!
   Wonderful news – have just received a letter from Kate to say that she'll be coming, and that you've invited her to stay at the Centre so as to save her pennies. If only I had a word from Ulrica I'd be over the moon. Can't think what's happened.
   Oh yes, and Metro Goldwyn is all set to stay at Raffles for a few days, and is *so* looking forward to long cosy chats – not if I see her first! I must say she was jolly patronizing about Clifford and the divorce, but then I find most married women seem to be the same, damn it. So typical, she laid the blame for our breakup on the schemings of a younger woman,

whereas, of course, it was just a drifting apart. We even write to each other now and then, though I must confess his letters are dreadfully dull. Still, Ben is devoted to him, though I wish he wouldn't ape his ways quite so much. Can't remember whether I mentioned or not that he's reading English and wants to teach – *Ben* not Clifford! It reminds me of when I was trying to teach the children in Camp Two. I shall never forget how furious you got when I told them Florence Nightingale was a saint, and you thundered back that she was nothing but a glorified plumber!

The flowers for Joss's grave sound perfect, though I can hear her shouting from the Beyond that it's a damned waste of money. Goodness how I miss her – more so now than ever before, can't think why. In fact, the other day I was on a bus passing through Holborn, when it stopped at the end of the street where she and Monica Radcliffe lived before the war. And guess what? I jumped off and went and stood outside number twenty-two, staring up at the top floor with the tears just streaming down my face. Passers-by must have thought I was barmy.

Dorothy has taken on the travel arrangements and will let you know in good time when we arrive. I must confess her secretary is so grand that she quite terrifies me. In fact, she makes me feel as if speaking to Miss Bennett (she's dropped the Mrs for work) is almost as much of an honour as being allowed to see Yamauchi in the camp office – how I used to quake before I went in.

Can't wait to see you and have a real heart-to-heart. Remember how we used to go to the latrines because it was the only place where we could ever be alone?

Take care of yourself, and don't work too too hard.

    Lots of love,
    Marion

Day later. Have just got back from seeing Alice and her father, Mr Courtenay. What a time I've had! Don't worry. Alice *is* coming, but oh dear! Her father is the over-protective type, who doesn't think it at all a good idea that his 'little girl' should remind to Singapore and be reminded of her mother's death and the dreadful times they went through. Not that Alice didn't, poor darling, but I'm sure it's better to face up to things, rather than to pretend they never happened.

Incidentally, something's not quite right with Alice. Can't put my finger on it, but she's still such a *child* – even looks one – and according to her father, finds it quite impossible to follow anything through. For instance, she got engaged to a very nice young man and then for no apparent reason suddenly broke it off at the very last minute – invitations had gone out and everything. But then, what she really needs is to have a good long chinwag with you, Oh Wise One. You were always so marvellous at understanding what made us tick – especially me!

Brick Lane,
Aldwych East,
East End,
London

2nd September, 1950

Dear Sis,

Many thanks for saying you'll come down and keep an eye on the kids. Not that Jim and his Mum won't cope, but it'll put my mind at rest if you're there as well. And more thanks for the thirty bob. I went straight off down to the market and blued the lot on a new frock for the reunion. It's pale blue with one of those stiff underskirts, but it doesn't half scratch the legs! Never mind, we all have to suffer to look presentable, and I don't want that old snob Van Meyer or whatever she's calling herself now, looking down her snooty nose. Not that she won't whatever I wear, the old cow.

Thanks for asking and baby's cough *is* a bit looser, but I dread the winter and all those fogs, and it's no joke having to wash him in the kitchen, what with the draught from under the yard door and the gaps in the window. (Council says we won't get a bathroom or indoor privy for at least two years would you believe, and as for re-housing!) Still, mustn't grumble, and Jim does his bit to help out, though he's dog tired when he does get in, which is always after eight what with his union work on top of his job. Not that I don't back him now the bloody Conservatives have reduced our lovely Labour majority. Still, at least we're in power for another four years – by the time it comes to the next election the bastards won't be able to unpick our welfare state even if they want to – and don't kid yourself, they're just biding their time, like the sneaky buggers they are.

Our Blanche is getting a proper little madam. Won't wear this, won't wear that. Yesterday, I found her up in our bedroom shuffling around in my high heels and with makeup all over her face and jumper. Oh yes, and last washday when I was up to my neck, she goes and cuts off her eyelashes!

Just wish my old mate Blanche could see her. Come to think of it *my* Blanche has taken after her in more ways than one, specially when it comes to the clobber. Honestly, the lengths big Blanche went to in camp to buy a right tatty number *and* it was too tight.(Shouldn't have said that, 'cos she gave it me last time she was put in the punishment cell – often thought she knew she was going to die.)

Last night my ma-in-law took me off to the local flea pit to see *The Winslow Boy*. We quite liked it but they made the Cockney sound so stupid it was like she was a music hall turn instead of a real person. Ma-in-law came stamping out saying they deserved to have their blocks knocked off! (As you're still such a Northerner, blocks means heads, only I remember you saying what a Cockney I'd become.)

Thanks again for everything, and don't forget to ask Jim for a shilling in case you need it for the meter when he's out. (Torch for the privy's in the drawer by the sink.)

> T.T.F.N. as I.T.M.A. would say,
> From your ever loving Sis,
> Maggie

P.S. Did you see about the United Nations debating Korea and how they'll knock some sense into them? Some hope! As Jim said at the last meeting of shop stewards, what's the point in having a United Anything when they don't have the clout, not having an army and the big powers with a veto. Bloody window dressing!

> Charles Street,
> Mayfair,
> London W1

> 5th September, 1950

Darling Charlotte,

Thanks for the super postcard, and I must say your grandfather's lodge sounds simply terrific. Fancy having a bath with wickerwork down the side, it must be as ancient as he is!

Poor Daddy's been going hammer and tongs, because I'm off to see some old friends in Singapore. You'd think I was going to the moon the way he carries on about the Emergency. You wouldn't believe the times I've had to remind him that there's *no* fighting in Singapore, and that the water is *quite* pure, and that I promise I won't go anywhere unescorted – if only he knew what we got up to in Zürich, he'd have a fit!

Buffer Simpson – the mousy boy with the heavenly voice we met at the Carmichaels – took me to the dance at Londonderry House. Can't tell you how simply marvellous the band was, but I'd better warn you, Buffer's N.S.T. so watch out!

Have just finished the *Gone with the Wind* you lent me. Goodness how I howled at the childbirth scene! Poor Melanie! If I ever have a baby I shall absolutely insist on being put under for the whole operation.

Will send you a jolly P.C. from Singapore to add to your collection, and if your father happens to drop in on Daddy, do ask him to say that the place is as safe as houses – if not safer considering the last do at James's. Honestly, *some people*!

Off to the dressmaker – so must fly – see you in Gunter's when I get back, when I'll *tell all*.

> Masses of love, etc.
> Alice

P.S. You'll never guess! Daddy's just come in with a solar topee he borrowed from my aunt. Even after I reminded him I'd spent simply years in the sun without a hat, he *insisted* I take it. Not to worry, I'll just leave it in some airport or other.

> Primrose Hill,
> London NW3

> 2 a.m.!

Darling Ben,
> Herewith your socks duly washed and darned!

Am off first thing, so this is a quick au revoir, and I also enclose a small cheque to help out with your text books. (Surely we have a Byron here, or did Daddy take it with him?)

Now don't forget, if you need to get hold of me urgently, you're to hang the cost and telephone Raffles; and if you run out of funds get hold of Uncle John who's had strict instructions to give you an advance, which you *must pay back* out of your next allowance.

Think of me sometimes, on this trip into the past, for I'm feeling very strange. Half of me as nervous as anything and the rest of me longing to see my old friends and hear all their news. (Haven't heard from Sister Ulrica yet, so keep your fingers crossed.)

As I'm sure I've told you more than once – don't be a bore, Mummy! – we were together so long and in such cramped quarters, that it'll be like remeeting bits of myself only once removed.

No, I'm not taking my dreadful old clothes, in fact I've quite splashed out, and have even had my hair 'styled' by Raymond – a very grand hairdresser in Dover Street who sports a red velvet jacket complete with carnation.

Much love, and remember to write to Granny and thank her for the pullover.

Loads of Love,
Mummy

P.S. I enclose some envelopes with the correct stamps for Singapore, so there's no excuse not to write!

2

Singapore

Doctor Beatrice Mason, healer of the sick and fighter against injustice, sucked an acid drop as she lay on her bed and waited for the dawn.

For the third night running she had dreamt she was back in Camp Two and the guards had set fire to the sick bay, the flames like great red hands reaching out to grab her as she ran across the compound and into Yamauchi's office. As always, he was staring out of the window with his back to the door, and when at last he turned round, she saw that he had the face of her father; and not just that, but she found herself shrinking into a little girl again and he was shouting at her, telling her she couldn't go out to play because she'd been rude to the Sunday school teacher.

Beatrice rolled on to her side, shoving a pillow over her head because of Stephen's snores from the next room.

To think that after all that's happened I'm still trying to escape, she brooded, wondering how it had been possible that such a little ninny as she'd been had managed to slip the reins of such a dominant Mr Know-all. Hard to credit that he now lay powerless to touch her, safe in the confines of the churchyard on the outskirts of Wolverhampton.

The Reverend Barnaby Charles Mason.
Beloved husband of Jane Mercia
and

Only son of Barnaby Harold Mason.
'He never did an unjust act.'

No, nor a spontaneous one either, not in all the nineteen years she'd been trapped within the echoing walls of that unlovely house. No Siree! Let not an undisciplined thought disturb such a powerplant of pious and ordered cruelty. Even now, the memory of when her father had discovered that she'd been seen with the Jones boy, had the power to send shivers through her.

'Beware the instincts,' he had thundered, his thin spatulate thumbs thrust sideways into the armholes of his waistcoat. 'Instincts, my girl, are but another name for Sin, that's what instincts are! To be routed out, mark me, and examined from every angle in the cold light of reason and the blessed words of the "Good Book".'

Small wonder she'd accepted hospital discipline and the bleak security of a fixed timetable, not to mention never risking the uncertainties of sharing her life with another man. Still, at least her father had spurred her on to throw off the God who had been such an ally in his battle for her angry and stubborn soul.

From the next room, the snores trembled into a wheezy splutter, followed by a creak of the bedsprings as Stephen heaved himself upright and spat.

How surprising life was, Beatrice decided for the umpteenth time, that it had taken imprisonment for her to learn finally to trust her feelings. Of course, originally it was the lack of medicines that had forced her to fall back on her insight, if only in a last desperate attempt to save those who still had a will to live. She smiled bleakly, for despite or perhaps *because* of all that had happened, it had certainly had its moments! Indeed, in some ways it had been more rewarding than much of the rest of her life: the close friendships, the sharing of each other's problems, and the small triumphs that they had celebrated with such joy. She and Marion and . . .

Beatrice sat up with a jerk. What on earth was she thinking of, when today was the day Marion and

Dorothy and Maggie and Alice were flying in from England! Groping for her spectacles and thrusting them up her nose, she peered at the still hazy outline of bedroom. In a few hours' time they'd be here, and there was still so much to be done. She pulled on her kimono, fiercely tying a knot as she tiptoed past Stephen's room in case he decided to get up and irritate her. 5.30 a.m.! Which meant that she could have a leisurely breakfast, followed by a good three hours' work sorting out the family planning clinic, then a quick sponge down and a change of clothes and off to the landing stage, to meet the flying boat. The simplicity of her morning delighted her, and she decided to spoil herself by opening the pot of Oxford marmalade she'd found in the new delicatessen in Malabar Street.

Armed with a mango and a mug of China tea, Beatrice descended the stairs to the ground floor. How cool it was in the Centre, and how serene without the endless jabber of all their clients, and what a long way they had come since that day in '45 when Joss and Stephen had opened the first Centre's doors to the refugees!

Beatrice crossed the hall and unlocked the doors into the courtyard, the dawn breeze cooling her face as the first rays of the sun streaked across the sky.

Resting her mug on the ledge of the schoolroom window, Beatrice sat on an upturned bucket, thinking how peaceful the city seemed without the traffic pounding past; and how it still, after all these years, had the power to surprise and delight her: the narrow streets with their houses still built to the same design as those of the early settlers; the exotic smells of the Arab, Indian and Chinese quarters; the broad avenues with their trishaws and cars that interwove like a ritual dance; and above all the lush vegetation that you could almost see sucking in the sun and the rains which fell with such a blessed regularity. Yes indeed, there were many worse places to live and die, she decided, easing her backside off the cutting edge of her seat, which for some reason reminded her of the latrines in camp.

The times she and Joss had sat side by side exchanging forbidden scraps of news, while her eyes – still just able to focus – had scanned the earth for snails and slugs, or indeed any moving thing that could be cooked and mashed into the patients' meals. Dear, irreplaceable Joss, how chuffed she would have been to see everything her money had achieved; the surgery, the mother and baby clinic, the Marie Stopes clinic, the administration office, and best of all the schoolroom named after her, and where Christina now taught with such diligent purpose.

'Penny for your thoughts?' Kate shouted, crossing the courtyard with long easy strides, and as brown and as healthy as five years of Australian weather and food could make her.

'Morning, Kate. Thought you'd still be sleeping off your flight.'

'On today of all days? You must be joking!'

Kate squatted on her haunches, her open and innocent face raised to the sun which was just topping the roof, its rays blazing on to the window panes which split them into diamonds of piercing light.

'Bea! I know that look. You were brooding on the camps, now weren't you?'

'Just about.'

'Me too. Hardly surprising considering.' Kate paused, drawing a stick man in the dust with the tip of her capable finger. 'You know the one I'm going to miss like billy-oh when we have our party?'

'Blanche?'

'Dead on. Keep on remembering what fun she was, and how gutsy – even to the very end.'

'As you say.'

Abruptly Beatrice turned her back, taking her anger out on Stephen by hollering up to his window.

'Wentworth! I know you're awake so stir your stumps. You've only five hours before everyone gets here, and I want you spruced up, and not in that pyjama top and those dreadful trousers, do you hear me?'

From the window, Kate watched a veined hand throw

a slipper in the direction of Beatrice's head. 'Spruce yourself up, you bossy old bag. I'll wear what I damned well like!'

'We'll see about that!'

Retying her kimono belt even tighter, Beatrice stamped back into the Centre, the slap slap of her slippers sharp on the stairs as she continued to shout up to her obstreperous partner.

What a comic pair they were, Kate thought. And how sad. For though Bea's letters had prepared her for the changes in both of them, it had still come as a shock.

Her plane had been late, and she'd run down the gangway almost hysterical with anticipation as she searched the crowd in front of the terminal. And then, just when she thought they'd forgotten her, she spotted them standing side by side staring towards the passengers still streaming off the airplane. Of course she'd prepared herself for Bea looking older, but not for the thickness of her spectacles, nor for the way she peered through them. And her body – that too had somehow aged, or was it perhaps that she was so used to the robust health of her compatriots? And then, poor old Stephen, who'd been hanging on to Bea's arms so that she couldn't make out who was helping whom, the skin of his face stretched tight across his nose, and the lines to his mouth like cracks in a rock, and his shoulders bent and the blades seeming like razors through the faded linen of his jacket. Damn it, she'd felt like a Peeping Tom catching them so unawares, but it had been even worse when she'd caught their attention and they had straightened their backs and beamed at her fit to bust.

Into her head had come the picture of two inmates of Belsen that she'd seen on a newsreel in Sydney. It had been part of a captured Nazi film, and a new intake was filing past a smart S.S. Commandant. The elderly couple were at the back, the man with a stick and the woman clutching his hand as if she might fall. As they drew level, they had straightened their backs, the same exaggerated smiles on their faces as they mouthed some pleasantries, while the commentator had remarked that when the officer waved them to the left it meant that they would be sent to the death camps.

Of course, the moment Stephen and Bea had greeted her the image had died, what with Bea's bubbling excitement, and even Stephen – who had to be reminded of who she was – getting in a sly dig about her peculiar accent. And then, when he'd suggested a drink and Bea had turned on him, she had seen that their relationship was still exactly the same: Bea domineering and Stephen deliberately setting out to goad her.

Even so, when they were in the taxi she had still felt uneasy, what with Bea fussing over her like some old hen, and saying that she must rest. How she had longed for the old Bea; the Doctor Mason as she'd first known her, when she'd been in charge of the ward and she was a raw nurse on her very first posting. What a battleaxe she had been with her certainty that nurses were there to do her bidding, or else! 'Nurse Norris, you're here to do things my way, not yours.' The times she'd been told that, and *how* she had hated her guts; had gone on hating her right through the first months in camp. And now? So compassionate and caring, and so proud that *her* nurse Norris would soon be a doctor and following in her footsteps.

Kate lifted her head and listened.

Beyond the walls, she could just hear the tinkling of bicycle bells as the first of the office workers peddled past the Centre. There they went zooming down the street, unaware of the old Tempei Kai interrogation centre where so many had been tortured and killed.

We're nothing but living ghosts, Kate thought, and in her mind's eye she saw the grave she'd visited the night before.

Dear, tragic Tom, who had survived all those years of internment, only to peg out a few months after the war had ended. And then, just a yard or so away, their splendid Joss, who was now nothing but a patch of earth and a headstone.

For a brief moment Kate envied them their state, if only because they no longer had to make up their minds about anything. Unlike her.

'Kate? Would you like some breakfast?'

Christina stood framed in the hall doorway, a neat slim figure wearing the traditional dress of the Straits-born Chinese, except that the colour was dowdier than usual; and with her hair scragged back into a bun, as if to deny the beauty that she had once confided was all that she had.

'Sure, Christina, I'd love some.'

Without waiting for Kate, Christina turned and went inside, and it was only on the stairs that Kate caught up with her old roommate from Raffles Hotel.

'Christina? Why don't you wear your hair down as you sometimes used to? It was so pretty.'

'Not practical. Surely you as a medical student must know that?'

'All I know is that I'm famished,' Kate laughed, but Christina did not respond.

The reception shed for the flying boat was as hot and as humid as the punishment hut, so that when the connection from London was announced, the waiting friends streamed out on to the jetty as if they were children who had suddenly been let out of school.

'There it is!' shouted Kate, pointing to the Sunderland as it hit the water, the waves spewing into twin arches of spray, while the blurred circles of its propellers slowly materialised into four separate fins.

Instinctively, the group from the Centre closed ranks as if their friends from London might find them wanting; and when finally the door of the flying boat opened, it was some seconds before they spoke. Again it was Kate who shouted: 'Look, there's Marion! And Dorothy and Maggie and Alice,' as she elbowed her way to the front of the crowd.

Stephen caught hold of Bea's arm to lead her forward, but she shook him off, standing her ground and waiting, so that she appeared almost austere as Marion rushed forward to greet her.

'Bea! Bea, it's *me!*'

Marion threw her arms round her old friend, the familiar smell of her hair, which was a combination of disinfectant and Greens soft soap, bridging the years as no amount of chatter could ever have done.

'And about time too.' Bea patted Marion's back, touching the bones of her spine and thinking that she was still too thin and would have to be fattened up.

And then it was all shouting and picking up cases and hurrying forward to get the formalities over. Except, that is, for Jake Haulter, who had just arrived, and who never liked to be seen hurrying anywhere. He stepped forward with an elegant grace as he picked up Maggie and Dorothy's luggage and marvelled at how pleased he was to see them. Especially Dorothy.

Surreptitiously, he glanced at her out of the corner of his eye. How very attractive she was, had always been really in an earthy and dangerous way. But now she was stunning, from the top of her shining hair to the tips of her elegant and expensive shoes. The little bitch had really made it! And what's more the challenge in her eyes told him that she knew it and revelled in the knowledge.

'Come on you two,' Jake shouted as he pushed through the throng. 'I know a man who'll get us through double quick, then it's into the car and Raffles here we come.'

'You haven't changed,' Maggie told him, wondering if he remembered how they'd made love, and whether he'd make a pass at her this time round? Not that she'd encourage him, of course, for she was now a married woman, but even so . . . However, it was Dorothy's knowing smile that Jake was watching.

All of the women agreed that Raffles had hardly changed since that never-to-be-forgotten day when R.A.P.W.I. had billeted them there after their release from camp.

It was a touch smarter perhaps, with a new coat of paint here and there, but in essence it had remained what it had always been: the most stylish hotel in Singapore or for that matter in the whole of the Far East; an institution that had ridden so many storms and changes that it had no need of updating and indeed took a pride in its faded and old world charm. There were the Tamils still running reception, and the Chinese waiters and boys moving as silently on slippered foot. Even the ceiling fans seemed to turn at a more leisurely pace, as if the air itself was somehow rarefied and had no need of too much disturbance.

Jake hung back at the entrance, watching the friends gather round the desks as they asked the hall porter if he'd received their booking?

How lucky they were to be able to bridge five long years so easily, he thought, when *he*'d never managed to be intimate with anyone. At least not since his great-grandfather. And for all its horrors, how he envied them their internment, if only that they seemed to accept each other for what they were; didn't always have to be one step ahead, and still never be able to let up. He pulled his cigarette case out of his pocket, staring at its smooth gold surface, before opening it with his thumb. Ah well, to each his own, *c'est la vie* and all that claptrap.

The head porter signalled to his assistant to fetch the keys, while assuring the friends that their rooms had been reserved, and that indeed one of their party had already booked in. 'A Mrs Forster-Brown.'

'Who?' Maggie demanded, and the porter was about to repeat himself, when the woman herself appeared. It was none other than Dominica, who sailed towards them like a plump little yacht, all sail and billow, with her hands held out in a dramatic gesture of welcome and that simpering smile that suddenly all her friends remembered so well.

In their surprise, Maggie and Dorothy had stepped back, watching with cynical eyes as Dominica gushed endlessly over Marion, while at the same time taking in Kate and Alice's reaction to her ladylike charm.

'Trust her to find a double barrel!' Dorothy remarked, noting with satisfaction that Metro Goldwyn had put on a great deal of weight, and that her clothes were neither as smart nor as expensive as her own.

'Your room is next to mine,' Dominica was reassured Marion with a knowing and intimate look. 'It's one of the best, and dear Alice is on the other side.' To which she added as an afterthought, that she wasn't too sure where they'd put Maggie and Dorothy, her tone condescendingly vague as she averted her eyes from Dorothy's model hat.

This was the moment Dorothy had been waiting for ever since she'd decided to come to Singapore – indeed it was one of the reasons she'd come at all. With a questioning lift of her eyebrows, she turned to the hall porter, who informed her that if she was a Mrs Dorothy Bennett accompanied by a friend, then they were in the very best suite – the Palm Court!

Dominica's smile was all the reward that Dorothy asked for, for it was as tight and as false as her hair of unnaturally brown curls.

'Come on, Maggie.'

And the ex-camp tart and her friend who had borne a bastard by an unknown soldier swept out of reception as if they were royalty.

Dominica sat on the bed watching Marion unpack, and she found it some comfort that their ex-leader looked so very much older – ten years at least if anyone had asked her – and her hair with those ugly streaks of grey. Not that it made up for Dorothy's appearance, nor her obvious wealth. How dare she and her common little friend make fun of her lovely new name. Oh yes, she'd heard them all right, but then they'd intended she would, which just went to show that they had no manners at all.

Not that those two had ever known how to behave!

Dominica's self-pity at the unfairness of life was so all-embracing, that for a moment she longed to be back with her dear Teddy, who adored the ground she walked on, and truly appreciated what a real lady she was. Honestly, it made her feel quite faint when she thought of what those two had got up to in camp. Especially that Dorothy, considering the way she'd sold herself to the guards, and the awful unspeakable things she'd done behind the huts. And what was so shocking was her lack of shame for the depths into which she had fallen. Even, now she thought about it, when that charming woman from Camp Two had arrived at Raffles, and recognised Dorothy and complained to Mrs Bristow. For once the stupid woman had done the right thing by sending Dorothy back to London, though why they had to send her by plane, when the rest of them were shipped off in boats, was quite another matter.

Too agitated to be able to sit still, Dominica crossed to the window, glaring down at a Malay who was weeding a window box of geraniums. Not that the rest of her friends had been much better, considering the excuses they had made for the bitch; especially Bea, who had had the cheek to tell them it was only because Dorothy had lost little Violet that she no longer cared how she behaved. After all, others had lost their babies, including poor innocent Sally, but *she* hadn't turned into a tart. Far from it. She'd done the sensitive thing and killed herself, which at least showed the depth of her feeling for her dead husband and still-born child, not to mention her loathing for those unspeakable Japs.

Dominica shifted her gaze back to Marion, again taking comfort in the changes in her appearance. 'You look older, Marion.'

'I am older.'

'Perhaps. But one must *not* give way to it.' Dominica lowered her voice and spoke with the delicacy that befits the wife of a Forster-Brown. 'I will let you into a secret. I give my hair a little help, and you Marion, should do the same.'

'Can't be bothered.'

Dominica sighed. If Marion couldn't even be bothered to look after her appearance, no wonder her handsome husband had run off with a younger woman. 'You must have been quite devastated when Clifford left you,' she remarked, noticing Marion's lipstick had smudged and that it wasn't a very becoming colour.

Damn and blast, thought Marion. Here we go again with all the same old explanations. 'He didn't leave me, Dominica. He met Angela after we'd separated, and the divorce was an *entirely* mutual decision.'

'Perhaps you'll find someone else, for at least you have good bones.'

Marion grabbed her sponge bag and headed for the bathroom, thinking that now she'd have to go through the same old rigmarole of how she was leading such a *very* full life with her friends, and of course Ben often came home for the vacs, so quite honestly she was hardly ever alone. And let's not forget her work, her oh-so-satisfying work for the Red Cross Library Service, and *no* she did not quite see herself marrying again. And she said all these things, and though Dominica did not for one moment believe her, even she hadn't the gall to press further.

'So, Dominica – tell me about *your* husband.'

'Dear Teddy! He is a *pet*, and so different from that creature I was married to before.'

Dominica was off, for there was nothing she loved better than talking about herself and those who loved her with such abandon. Eyes sparkling, she told how, after Van Meyer had died, she had returned to Singapore to look up dear Colonel Jackson who had been so in love with her, and how the Army had most inconsiderately posted him to India of all places! Not that it hadn't been for the best, for she had met her own dear Teddy at the Seaview Hotel, and it had been love at first sight for both of them.

As she spoke of her husband, her face softened, and Marion saw that she was indeed in love. In fact, she was strangely moved by Metro's tenderness, for however maddening she'd been in the camps, they would always be close because they *had* been there, whatever they felt about each other as people.

'Everything would be perfect, Marion, but for those damned Communists. But as I have so often said to my Teddy, if the Japs didn't scare me to death, then I'm not going to let a lot of stupid natives get rid of me now.' And Metro lifted her head into the arrogant pose that she favoured when making a statement of some importance, and Marion saw that indeed she had meant every word she had said.

In the adjacent room, Beatrice was only half listening, as Alice chattered on about her life in London; and how, now that she'd broken off her engagement, she was thinking she might do a First Aid course, or perhaps work for some charity or other, or then again she could travel a bit because Daddy gave her an allowance, and now she was twenty-one – nearly twenty-two actually – it was always a jolly good thing to broaden one's horizons, don't you think?

Hell's bells, thought Beatrice, will the girl never shut up? But then she was always irritable when she was having a bout of depression. To think that all those years of experience would soon go to waste just because of a few bloody years without vitamin B. It was ridiculous. Not that she wouldn't fight it all the way, and at least none of them realised how close to blindness she really was. Until the photograph. Not that she hadn't managed to cover up, but for how much longer?

Finding her way to Alice's room had been a piece of cake. After all, she knew the layout of the hotel almost as well as her Centre. In fact she had been feeling quite chuffed with herself because she'd managed to sit on Alice's bed without first feeling for the edge, and how was she to know that she'd been staring at Mrs Courtney's photograph?

If it hadn't been for Alice remarking 'It's Mummy', she'd never have known what to say. As it was, instead of replying 'I know', she'd muttered 'What?' like some sort of blithering idiot. Still, the child hadn't seemed to notice, for she had chatted on about how it'd been taken before the war, and how her father had said that was the way he'd like his daughter to remember her mother. Not that she could. In fact she couldn't remember her in the camps at all, and everything before that was a bit of a blur.

'Beatrice, may I ask you something?'

Beatrice pulled herself together and tried to sound interested.

'Fire away.'

'When Mummy was dying you kept me out of the way, but now I'm no longer a child, and I need to know. *All* the details. What she said. How she felt. *Anything.*'

Beatrice felt herself blushing in sheer panic. How could she tell Alice about the death of her mother, when she was hopeless at names and couldn't even identify the woman from a photograph? So she fell back on a half-truth, though most of the hundreds of deaths were etched into her memory by an anger that still had power to burn.

'Oh, my dear, I can't remember the details. There were so many deaths that each ran into the other.'

'Oh. Yes, of course.'

'Your Mother? Tell me what did she die of?'

'More or less everything.'

Beatrice nodded her head, remembering the hopelessness of the sick bay: no bandages, hardly any water, no food to speak of, and worst of all no medicines, because Yamauchi and the guards wouldn't allow them their Red Cross parcels, even though they were stacked in the storehouse and hadn't been touched. If they had looted them, then that at least would have been human and she wouldn't have minded so much, but to lock the door on them for the duration! She could have forgiven the Japs many things, but never that.

Beatrice stood up and made for the door, which she'd counted as five paces. 'Must go and find out what Stephen is up to, or he'll be sneaking into the bar. Oh, and Alice, don't forget: drinks here this evening, then tomorrow Kate's picking you all up to bring you down to the Centre.'

'Super.'

Beatrice smiled in the direction of Alice's voice.

'It's lovely to see you.'

Driving back to his flat in Farquar Street, Jake felt on top of the world. he'd enjoyed having a sneaky drink with old Stephen who, despite his failing memory and shaky condition was always good for a gossip about local mismanagement, and on occasion could be extraordinarily perceptive about world conditions. Take his remarks about Korea: 'You mark my words, from now on the West'll choose the side they back according to their commercial interests – not that they haven't before. But the age of moral indignation is over, my boy – not that they won't trot it out whenever it suits them.' And he'd been very funny about Maggie and the way she'd shown off about the kids, even giving a suggestive nudge to show that he remembered that they'd once had a bunk-up.

Dear Maggie. She deserved her happy marriage and children, but must she be so very domestic with her talk of babies and housing conditions, and how rationing had got even worse? Hard to believe she'd ever been a little raver; had once dressed up in his dinner jacket and done a wicked take-off of the snobs who'd flooded into Raffles the moment that peace had broken out. And were still there, come to that. But then wasn't life in the East always a bugger's muddle what with all the layers of class and colour: white working-class Maggie; and him a half-caste, with a Swiss passport and a half-English father and Indian mother, though still of course a public school boy and all *that* implied! Small wonder they'd gravitated together, if only to share their chips on the shoulder about a system that had made them both such reluctant outsiders.

And then there was Dorothy. The unknown quantity.

He'd always lusted after her, ever since that day when he'd taken her to the godown to choose some furniture for her bungalow. He grinned as he remembered the girls – for that's what Maggie and Dot had been – still scabby and thin from the camps, and in those appalling clothes issued by that pompous Mrs Bristow of R.A.P.W.I., who had always been so over-polite whenever she'd met him.

How amazingly fast Dot had caught on to his suggestion that she choose antiques rather than something more functional.

'If the people who owned them are dead, why then you can flog the stuff,' he had told her, and she'd done just that. More, actually, for over the weeks she'd systematically picked his brains, even borrowing books on antiques, and combing the markets for any looted pieces small enough to pack in her case and sell when she got back home. And more power to her! All of a piece was Dot. A little survivor and grafter, just as he was.

Which reminded him. What with the trouble up-country and the rumour that Chinese Communists were planning to move into Tibet, he'd better transfer some more dollars before the currency fell even further.

Jake parked his car outside his flat and locked it with care, an alert slim figure in a Shantung suit, his dark skin and hair melting into the crowd as they hurried to be home before dark.

3

Marion woke with a hangover, feeling a not unpleasant languor, but with a pounding within her skull as if it had shrunk and was too small to contain her thoughts.

She opened her eyes, the shafts of light through the shutters enlarging what looked like ants on the tips of her eyelashes. *Ants?* Good God, she hadn't even washed off her make-up!

Marion sat up with care, gingerly lowering her legs to the floor and waiting for a moment before crossing to the basin and staring at the clown in the glass: hair like Medusa; lipstick wandering down to her chin; and the new mascara she had bought with such daring, now beaded into stiff black spikes.

She washed and towelled her face dry with some severity, telling herself that if she didn't watch out she'd be back to square one taking nips between meals, just as she had when her marriage was falling apart. Not that last night had been the same thing at all!

They had sat up late talking of old times and catching up with each other's news, and when she had finally come up to her room she had felt much too invigorated to sleep, and had rung for the waiter to bring her a gin sling. And then another. It had been a wonderful self-indulgence to sit by the window and drink herself into a mindless euphoria, for the heady mixture of heat and shared memories had reawakened inside her a feeling that she had believed was long gone. She couldn't quite put her finger on it, didn't wish to in case it would disappear, but it was there nevertheless: the old excitement of not knowing what the next moment would bring, and which, in a few short hours had unpicked the routine of her so carefully constructed life since the war.

Again she regarded herself in the glass, desperately trying to gauge the outward changes the years had wrought. Obviously she could never hope to be another Dorothy, who now looked younger than when she had been sent back to London with such indecent haste. Still, at least she could do her best.

Marion fetched her face cream and massaged it into her skin just as she'd seen it done on the films, though she felt a bit silly while she did so. Never mind, it was all in a good cause, and for once she would take her time over her makeup, before putting on her new Liberty's dress which had been such an extravagance because Clifford's allowance didn't allow for luxuries, especially now Ben was up at Oxford and continually overspending. Still, she didn't regret lashing out, not a bit of it. It was like being a schoolgirl again with no responsibilities except to herself. Hurrah!

Marion pulled the much-too-expensive dress out of the wardrobe, but instead of putting it on, she cast it aside, crossing to the window and pushing open the shutters.

Below her, Singapore shimmered in the mists of the morning heat, two rickshaws bowling along Beach Road as fast and as bright as children's hoops. She knew they were having a race for the occupants were egging on their runners, whose heads were bent so low that they seemed to grow out of their shoulders, the fast rhythm of their feet like clockwork mice, appearing and disappearing from under the edges of their straw hats. In and out, in and out they went, until the rickshaws sped past and all that was left were the backs of the faded awnings and the wheels spurting up feathers of dust.

Poor overworked devils. What a life it must be to run

round within the circle of the city as if they were dogs turning a spit, and their overlords accepting everything as if it was theirs by right! And for what? A pittance that would hardly keep themselves let alone their families.

At least I know what it's like, she thought, for hadn't they too been treated as a lower order, because women prisoners were beneath *all* men, and their only role was to obey those who had liberated the East from the white oppressor.

And now? Who was oppressing whom now? After all, unlike the rest of the Empire, the Sultans had *asked* the British to take over, or so she'd been told. God, the endless evenings when Clifford had lectured her about how there had been no standing army because Malaya had not been taken by force, and how that had been part of the trouble when the Japs invaded from the land. But now . . . ? After all that had happened, the country was still tearing itself apart; and all because a few couldn't wait for independence which surely would be given before much longer? 'Given.' The word echoed back to her with a bitter taste. Perhaps *that* was what the fighting was all about? Perhaps . . .

Marion Jefferson! You've no time to waste brooding about the past, when today was going to be absolutely jampacked, what with the visits to the Centre and Joss's grave, and then lunch in a street café *and* an afternoon's sightseeing, before a party which would no doubt go on well into the small hours.

Marion shook out her dress and slipped it on, trying to renew her pleasure in it, as she twirled in front of the glass and thinking she looked like some mechanical ballerina on the top of a musical box.

'Watch the birdie!' Dorothy pushed the button of her new Leica camera, before winding on the film.

On the way to the Centre, they had stopped at the Chinese market which was as noisy and as boisterous as a circus. On either side a jumble of stalls displayed their wares under cotton and bamboo canopies, or even the new plastic material; while wandering through the crowd, Malays, Chinese, Indians, White Russians and half-caste traders carried trays of matches, curry puffs, fried fish, herbal cures and smuggled American cigarettes so essential to casual passers-by.

Kate had not wanted to stop, in fact she had become quite stroppy, but the rest – Marion, Dorothy, Maggie, Alice and Dominica had insisted, if only to buy some presents to take back home; and besides, they couldn't resist the sheer liveliness of the place.

'Say cheese,' Dorothy shouted to Marion and Dominica, Marion smiling self-consciously, while Dominica arranged her face into a simpering smile; afterwards turning to Marion and remarking how lucky she was to have such photogenic bones, and offering her a bag of pink and white Turkish Delight. Marion shook her head, desperately trying not to giggle; for with a sweet in both cheeks, Metro looked exactly like Ben's much-loved hamster, Bessie Braddock, who had come to such an untimely end when he had gnawed through the telephone flex.

'No thank you, Dominica, not after my enormous breakfast.'

'I too should not eat between meals, but snacks are such a comfort when one spends one's days waiting for a husband who might never return!'

Immediately, Marion felt ashamed of herself, even while she was perfectly aware that whatever the subject, Metro would always find some way of leading it back to her suffering self.

From across the street, Alice was shouting and jumping up and down as she pointed to a bric-à-brac stall. 'Look, Dorothy, here's some ivory! Didn't you say you wanted some?'

'Honestly, Alice, not *that* junk,' Dorothy shouted with severity. 'Eighteenth-century netsuke is what I'm after.'

Marion watched them as they turned over the trinkets: Dorothy so sophisticated, while beside her Alice looked almost gauche, which was probably why she felt such a wave of tenderness for her. So young to have been through so much – no wonder she couldn't remember her mother in the camps.

Not that Marion could remember much about Mrs Courtney herself, except that she and Alice had been very close; that Sarah Courtenay was one of those seemingly passive women who could hold a child in a web of unspoken needs that was so much stronger than many a direct demand – if only for being oblique; and which had made Alice's reaction to her mother's death so very disturbing.

They had expected Alice to be devastated, but instead she hadn't even cried, only wandering about the camp and telling anyone who had tried to sympathise that she was quite all right, thank you, and please riot to make so much fuss.

'Come *on*, Dozy Drawers, we're nearly there and Bea'll be champing at the bit.'

Kate grabbed Marion's arm and pulled her through the crowd, and it reminded Marion of how Bea had often grabbed her in just the same way. But then, wasn't it natural for Kate to have picked up some of Bea's ways, for in the last year of internment she had been like a daughter to her, what with deciding to follow in Bea's footsteps and become a doctor, and Bea so very proud that she had been the one who had helped Kate to make her decision.

'So how's the studying, Kate?'

'Don't! Four years down and three to go – feels like forever.'

They turned off the busy street and suddenly, there in front of them was a large and impressive board proclaiming 'Monica Radcliffe Foundation and Welfare Centre'.

'Here we are,' Kate announced in a mock tourist-guide voice, as she gestured towards the building which was painted mustard yellow, with a low wall around the courtyard. 'You see in front of you the now famous Centre, with its . . .'

Marion stared at its solid bulk, which was in such contrast to the first Centre which had been in a disused temple and had been lent by some Buddhist monks, who had asked nothing in return except that it might help the poor of their war-torn city.

The Monica Radcliffe Foundation and Welfare Centre! What a splendid ring it had to it, and to think that the woman after whom it was named had died in an unknown camp, years before even the idea of helping the refugees had been thought of; a woman none of them had even met and yet felt that they knew as intimately as their closest friend.

Monica Radcliffe. The woman who had shared her life with Joss ever since the 1890s, when they had both been students at Cambridge. Marion smiled to herself at the picture the pair must have made: Monica so short and fierce, and Joss as tall and as thin as a stork, and with that childlike curiosity that is only given to those who have never considered themselves.

During the long evenings in camp, how Joss had enthralled them with the stories of what she and Monica had got up to: their trips on the motorbicycle, Joss sporting a leather helmet and goggles and Monica riding pillion; their endless campaigns when they were suffragettes and had both suffered imprisonment and the terrible force-feeding; their work in the soup kitchen during the General Strike; their marches through the East End when they had joined the Socialists and Communists to protest against the Mosley gangs; and their epic journey to the Deep South of America to march with the poor Whites. What a record! And then, when they had been working with the Quakers helping refugees from the Spanish Civil War, Monica had suddenly taken it into her head to up and off to the East in order to start a school for the poor of Shanghai.

What a Madcap Maisie she must have been, Marion decided, remembering Joss boasting that Monica had even charged into the brothels informing the prostitutes that their children had just as much right to an education as anyone else in Shanghai! It must have been around that time that Monica had first met Stephen, for she had bullied him into being a part-time English teacher – despite his protests that he needed all the time he could get in order to write The Definitive Novel. Not that he ever had, bless him, having moved on to a full-time teaching post in Singapore, which was when – according to Joss – Monica had telegraphed her cry of help, and Joss had dropped everything and rushed out to join her.

It seemed incredible to Marion that Joss and Stephen had never met until that fateful day some weeks after they'd been liberated. Poor Stephen had been wandering around Raffles asking everyone if they had any news of a Monica Radcliffe who'd been interned on one of the islands, and Joss had happened to overhear. Not that their meeting had begun auspiciously, for it had been Joss's sad task to break Monica's death to him, and it was only after that that they had discovered who the other one was.

How very typical of Monica, that over the years she had written endlessly to Joss about the paragon of a teacher she had found, while at the same time chastising Stephen that he wasn't a patch on her splendid chum back home! Just as now, Stephen constantly reminded Bea how *very* splendid his dear and much lamented Joss had been.

But of course, thought Marion, amazed that she had never seen it before! Stephen, the seemingly passive drifter, *he* had been the one to choose the women – not the other way round – remorselessly weaving them all into the chain of his needs: Monica, Joss and now Bea; all of them women who had insisted on carrying him with them, unaware that that was the direction in which he had wanted to go anyway! Or as their link had once put it with such phoney displeasure: 'It's my lot in life to always end up with a bossy female!'

'Marion,' Kate yelled impatiently, 'come and join us!

I want you to meet Lau Peng, Bea's and Christina's right-hand man!'

'Hallo, Marion, I've heard so much about you.'

As much as any European can ever tell the age of an Asian, Marion decided that Lau Peng was about thirty-five years old, and with the neat movements that are a hallmark of the Chinese; though even for that good-natured race, he smiled more broadly and emphatically than any Chinaman she had ever encountered, the smile only shifting when Dorothy spotted the graffiti someone had chalked on the wall.

'My God, has *nothing* changed?' Dorothy demanded in disgust, pointing at the scrawled: 'White Men Go Home' and above it, 'Death to the Running Dogs'.

All the women had turned, their chatter dying in mid-sentence as they remembered the slogans that had greeted them on their first day back in the city after the camps; one or two of them glancing at Dorothy who had returned to her bungalow, only to find it looted of everything and covered, inside and out, with obscene slogans.

It was Alice who broke the silence. 'What does it mean, "Running Dogs"?' Lau Peng drew himself up, his voice rising in fury as he explained that it was the Communists' name for those like himself and Christina who had always given their wholehearted support to the British. Not that the majority of Chinese didn't feel the same, he added; and Marion remembered that the Chinese had stood by them all through the occupation; had taken the brunt of the Japanese brutality, right from the first days when thousands had been massacred and their bodies thrown into the harbour until it had clogged with their corpses.

Shouting to a workman to clean off the offensive scrawls, Lau Peng turned back to the visitors, passionately informing them that it was not the Communists but the people like him and Christina who *really* cared about the people of Malaya, for their work at the Centre was to teach the population to stand on their own two feet so that they'd be ready for independence when it finally came! Adding, again with mounting fury, that all the so-called liberators had to offer was their own filthy brand of terrorist imperialism; and as for Communist China . . .

Much to everyone's relief, his outburst was cut short by a cheery and familiar 'Good morning' from above their heads.

Beatrice was leaning over the balcony, and with ill-concealed pride demanded to know what they thought of the place? Though before they had the chance to tell her, she was shouting that they should just wait until they had seen the inside!

And indeed the inside was very impressive, though when they were shown into the waiting room, Dominica let out a tut-tut of disapproval because of the posters warning against venereal disease, even drawing her skirt aside when she passed any of the patients waiting for the surgery to open.

'They've not all got the pox, you know,' Dorothy told the fastidious Metro, eyeing an ivory carving hanging from an old man's belt. To which she added with glee that many of the Dutch girls in camp had had it, or had Metro forgotten the two who'd opened a brothel in Lavender Street and passed it on to their fine British Tommies?

'And I'm sure *that* is something you would know all about!' Dominica flung at her, but Dorothy was now talking to the old man and pretended not to hear her.

Smirking at the quickness of her response, Dominica turned to Bea, gushing in delight at how simply perfect everything was, and how had she done it, and hadn't she worked herself into the ground, and no wonder she looked so very worn out!

Poor Beatrice, who had vowed that this time she would *not* let Metro get under her skin, now found herself pontificating on how there was still more disease than anyone could possibly cope with; that most of *her* patients lived and starved in absolute squalor, indeed some of them living eight or more to a room! But Dominica was not to be put down, informing Beatrice that they too had suffered just the same in the camps, in fact worse, come to think of it, for at least the shops were now overflowing with good food.

Despite herself, Beatrice could hear the hysterical note in her voice as she snapped back that the food was there only for those who could afford it, and that most of her patients were out of work thank you very much, and on top of which the population was growing at a simply alarming rate, and just you try and interest *anyone* in such a new-fangled idea as birth control.

At the hint of sex, Dominica's mouth primped into a moue of distaste, and Beatrice strode into her office, grimly telling herself that in a changing world some things remained unchanged. Metro especially!

'This,' announced Beatrice, now thoroughly worked up, 'is where I do my interviews, and where Stephen spends most of his time getting my files in a muddle – when of course he is not on the bog where he spends most of the rest of his life!'

As if by magic, the victim of her outburst appeared in the doorway. 'And precious wonder the muck she feeds me!' he informed his audience, before giving them the well remembered and quizzical smile, his clothes now back to their usual eccentric mixture of pyjama top and scruffy ill-fitting trousers that ended way above his ankles.

'Can't eat this, can't eat that, don't drink too much. I tell you I lie in bed dreaming of stengahs and curry puffs,' he ended, his long arms waving his displeasure, and so thin that they might have belonged to a scarecrow, which in many ways he resembled.

'Perhaps that's what makes you snore,' Beatrice spat back at him, glancing at her friends to make quite sure that they'd registered how much she had to put up with.

'I do not *snore*.'

'Oh no? Then you should just try sleeping in the next room!'

'They go on like this all the time,' Kate whispered to Marion, who had been thinking that if she closed her eyes it could have been Stephen and Joss having one of their regular barneys.

When Beatrice suggested they all move on to the schoolroom to find Christina, Maggie hung back to wait for Dorothy, who was obviously up to her old tricks, for she was now holding the old man's carving and examining it with some satisfaction.

'Dot? How much did you pay for it?'

'M.Y.O.B.'

'Peanuts, I bet.'

'*He*'s not complaining!' And indeed the old man seemed delighted with the transaction.

'My God, Dot, but you can be ruthless!'

'No. Just a good businesswoman. And besides, if I hadn't got it someone else would have, so it makes no odds.'

'Bloody capitalist.'

'Listen, Maggie, there's only two kinds of people in this life: the givers and takers, and I'm . . .'

'One of the takers.'

Maggie felt herself shaking with the injustice of it, and not least because Dorothy was her friend. But then, wasn't Jim right when he'd told her that money was power, and always corrupts. How many times had she watched him thump the table, warning her that no battle was ever won, even now they had got a Labour Government. 'The bastards are just lying low, you mark my words,' he had told her over and over again. 'And one day they'll grab the reins back, and then there'll be trouble; especially for the likes of you and me, and all the others who've given their lives for something better.'

Suddenly realising that she was alone and that the patients were staring at her with ill-concealed curiosity, Maggie trailed out and followed the voices of her friends.

If only Joss were here, she'd have understood how she felt. And she thought of the day that Joss – hair on end from her bath – had stood in their room at Raffles, spluttering with rage at the Red Cross newspaper they had been issued by Mrs Bristow, who had explained that it had been printed to bring the prisoners up-to-date on what had been happening since they'd been captured. How indignant Joss had been at the way the paper had been slanted, it even implying that the Labour Party had only just got in. 'It was a landslide!' she'd shouted at them, clutching the towel around her bean-pole figure. And later, with a few drinks under her belt, she'd taken great delight in informing stuffy Major Jackson that although all the parties had agreed that they wouldn't contest Churchill's seat, an Independent had still stood against him, on the platform of a one-day working week! 'And would you believe, he managed to grab about eleven thousand votes out of something like thirty-six!' she had ended with malicious triumph.

Bugger Dorothy and her money, Maggie muttered, entering the schoolroom named after the friend that she missed so dreadfully.

The room had an old-fashioned air, with its rows of school desks, and the children in pinafores with their hands neatly folded as they listened to Christina giving a geography lesson. Behind her a large pre-war map of the world had been pinned to the wall, a fifth of its surface coloured a pretty shade of pink to distinguish the British Empire on which the sun was now so very definitely setting.

'Excuse me, Christina,' Beatrice interrupted tentatively, for Christina – who must have been aware of her friends – had continued to lecture the children on the recent independence of India. 'Our visitors are here.'

Dorothy watched Christina with mounting irritation, until at last she turned and greeted them; Dorothy refusing even to reply. Not yet another do-gooder! Jesus, when she thought of Christina as she'd first known her; little Miss Wouldn't-say-boo-to-a-goose, who, even in camp, had somehow managed to look like a girl, with her slick hairstyle kept up by those silly bits of bamboo, and the dress that was almost respectable because Madam worked in Yamauchi's office instead of labouring like the rest of them.

The resentment of those years rose afresh, as Dorothy remembered Christina's skin which had hardly had a blemish until the end; and how were they to know that Yamauchi was giving her titbits because of his more-than-deserved ulcer? All right, so they *had* accused her of collaborating, of informing on Rose and getting her shot, but why hadn't she tried to justify herself? Or had she been too ashamed of her sneaking liking for the bastard? And now look at her! Just a grey little schoolmarm, right down to the dreary clothes; and as for her lecturing them just like that boring Lau Peng! Surely she didn't have to launch into a bloody speech at their very first meeting!

'. . . so much illiteracy, especially for the Chinese. And now, thanks to the bandits, it's worse than ever because teachers trained in China have been barred, so there's *no* teaching in Chinese except for me and a few others, so what chance have our people of getting any kind of decent job? I get *so* angry at times, and so does Lau Peng.'

Dorothy shoved a cigarette into a holder which had been a present from her lover in London. Was there no end to the worthiness of Bea's helpers with their oh-so self-righteous smugness?

Dear Sister Ulrica had never been like that, but then she had been *really* good. And it came to Dorothy that they'd hardly mentioned Ulrica since they'd arrived in Singapore; that they hadn't even discussed why she hadn't replied to Marion's letter, hadn't been heard of for months, ever since she'd left the leper colony and gone to work for some Mission in the north.

Not that she didn't know why. They all thought that Ulrica was dead, shot by some bloody underground sniper, or blown sky high by one of their grenades.

The pain Dorothy felt was almost physical and she

stubbed out her cigarette, unconsciously hiding it in the palm of her hand as she'd done in the camps.

What a joke she and Ulrica must have been to the rest, Dorothy thought with some bitterness. The tart and her best friend the nun! Talk about chalk and cheese. Not that their differences had ever seemed to bother Ulrica; but then, she had been a real Christian, never preaching or even showing her disapproval, except when it came to the abortion. Even then Ulrica had stood by her, once she'd understood that nothing she said would make the least bit of difference. And afterwards, when she'd been so ill in the sickbay, it was Ulrica who had saved her life. She remembered how everything had seemed so unreal, with sounds coming at her as if from a long way off, and nothing in focus except for Ulrica's eyes, and so full of love that she had felt herself literally dragged back from the dead; pulled, hand over hand, up the strong rope of Ulrica's faith.

Dear God, please, *please* let her be alive somewhere. Let her be busy, stamping about in her habit and telling everyone what's what, and beaming like the darling she was.

4

Singapore

The Lady Jocelyn Holbrook
1870–1945
'Fight the good fight'

Of the hut in Camp Two, only those around Joss's grave had survived: Marion, Beatrice, Dorothy, Kate and Dominica, for Alice and Maggie, who stood with them, had joined the women when they had been sent to a prison camp after Yamauchi had discovered them looting the stores.

Where are they buried, Marion wondered? All the dear good friends she had known? In what ugly fastness did they lie, their home-made crosses long decayed and the blessed ground now smothered in undergrowth?

Again she felt her anger at the indifference of the Foreign Office and the War Graves Commission. Ah! the War Graves he had said, but we are only responsible for those who have served in the Forces. But hadn't the civilians served in their own way, just like the soldiers? The doctors like Bea, and the nurses like Kate and the long-dead Nellie, who had missed the chance of evacuation because they had refused to leave the patients to the mercy of the enemy. For that was what had been planned: the wounded and dying abandoned except for the few native nurses and doctors and the dead piled high in the side wards.

And then there were the other women: the midwives,

missionaries, drivers, teachers, charity workers, and the housewives and bar girls who had buckled to and taken on any job once Singapore was being besieged.

Again Marion was back in the shambles of the harbour during the last days: the blast of the bombs topping the never-ending gun fire, the shouting and screaming; the terrified population pushing its way towards the over-laden ships where soldiers had been posted on deck, using the butts of their rifles to thrust away any who had managed to clamber up the sides. A few who were lucky had fallen back on to the quay, while the rest had plummeted into the water or been crushed between iron and stone.

And there, in the dead centre of the chaos, a nurse – her uniform ingrained with filth and blood – edging a car full of wounded towards the nearest ship. Later, Marion had been told that it was the harbour master who had persuaded the nurse that her patients would have a better chance of survival ashore; that if they allowed any more on the ships, they would most likely sink where they lay. So she had returned back through the bombing to an empty maternity centre, where she had laid her patients under the beds, which she had piled high with corpses to give protection from the blast and the falling timber.

Where was she now, that dumpy middle-aged nurse?

For pity's sake, thought Marion, staring at and then through Joss's gravestone, if the Dutch could rebury their civilian dead in cemeteries, then why on earth couldn't we British?

Marion's eyes focused, as again she read the epitaph. 'Fight the good fight.' And she nodded her agreement, remembering a conversation she and Bea had overheard when they'd been waiting to embark on a ship to go home. It had been two sailors who had ranted on about how they could have been demobbed if it hadn't been for shipping back the spoilt darlings who'd sat on their arses drinking, rather than be evacuated like the rest. And who could blame them? No one was going to broadcast how or why they'd stayed on. Better to forget the whole business, leave it in the small print of an official report, bury it deep in the archives of some War Museum where it would do the least harm.

But I, thought Marion, I am a living witness. And the knowledge strengthened her determination to continue to fight for the women who could no longer fight for themselves.

It had been during her imprisonment in the camp that Marion had discovered an aggression that she had never dreamt she possessed; and which, together with her new-found independence, Clifford had found so shocking that it had led to the breakup of their marriage.

How sad it was, Marion brooded, that the memory of their loved ones, that had so sustained the women in camp, had so often foundered when they had finally come face to face.

She glanced across at Kate who was standing by the grave of her fiancé, Tom. She stood as if frozen, and Marion wondered what she was seeing with those wide and seemingly innocent eyes.

Kate's thoughts were very painful to her, not least because she was riddled with remorse. How cruel that Tom had somehow survived the war, only to end up in hospital, and with a fiancée who no longer wanted to marry.

To this day, she still wasn't sure if Tom had known how she felt, for the day before he'd died he had opened his eyes, had even managed a half-smile as he'd whispered through cracked lips that perhaps everything was for the best. She had felt so guilty that she had never told anyone, not even Bea. After all, *he* hadn't changed. He'd gone on wanting what they both had wanted – marriage and children – ever since he had proposed during those terrifying let's-live-now days before the fall of Singapore.

The *'Fall.'* The word made her think of the garden of Eden, where Eve had tempted Adam. Had it been *her* fall from grace, that during the years of internment, marriage had come to seem so restricting; that the fight to keep the patients alive had somehow given *her* much more life as well? She could still feel the moments of triumph when a so-called dying woman had pulled through and recovered. Dear God, it had been as heady as any drug, and she had fed on it, had gone on feeding on it right through her first years of study. But now? How did she feel now . . .

'Miss Norris, isn't it?'

Kate turned and saw a sandy-haired man of about thirty-five, his hands hanging loose by the sides of his scruffy trousers, and his face staring at her expectantly.

'You won't remember me, but I was working at the Alexander Hospital in '45. I knew your fiancé. Doctor Fraser's the name. Duncan Fraser.'

For a second Kate couldn't place him, until a picture came into her head of a P.O.W. sitting beside a patient in the next bed to Tom's, and who listened with grave concern as the man ranted deliriously. She remembered thinking how gentle he was, and how she would have liked just such a person to be beside her if she had been ill.

'Of course! Doctor Fraser. You'd just come out of Changi.'

'That's right.' He shifted from foot to foot, as if Changi was something of an embarrassment; so to fill in the pause, Kate asked him if he was still working at the hospital, and he told her he was, that he'd thought of going back to Scotland, but . . . He nodded towards a grave on which was inscribed 'Soo-Min Fraser. 1912–1943'.

'My wife was killed by the Japs for helping the British.' Then, as if the very mention of his bereavement was even more of an embarrassment, he hurried on to ask Kate why *she* had come back, and she found herself telling him all about the reunion and how she was staying with Doctor Mason at the Centre, and did he know Stephen Wentworth?

'Stephen was also at Changi, and besides I work at

the Centre part time. Anyway, everyone knows the Mole and the Matchstick!' he added with a grin; and because it was such a marvellously apt description, Kate found herself laughing out loud.

Dominica opened her eyes, for she had been praying for Joss's soul. She was deeply shocked. Honestly, these colonials had absolutely no idea how to behave; but then Kate had always been very thick-skinned – you had only to look at the way she had treated her on the many occasions when she was dying!

Dominica turned to Dorothy, remarking in hushed tones that she was *most* surprised that Kate could laugh when she was standing in front of her dead fiancé.

'Oh, for Christ's sake, would you rather she cut her throat?' Dorothy flung at her, before striding over to Maggie with the same angry stomp she had had when a guard had refused her offer to go behind the huts.

There is no shame in the creature, thought Dominica, beside herself with indignation as she looked around for someone with whom she could share her outrage. Sadly, her only witness was Alice, who was staring into the distance as if she hadn't heard a word; so Dominica raised her voice, announcing in ringing tones that for all Dorothy's finery she was still nothing but a foul-mouthed slut.

Ever the peacemaker, Marion hurried over to ask if they hadn't all better be going, but Dominica refused to answer. As far as she was concerned she wasn't at all sure that she shouldn't get on the next train back to Teddy, who understood how sensitive she was, and how upsetting it was for her to associate with anyone as vulgar and cheap as that Dorothy Bennett.

Marion sighed. If she didn't watch out, the day they had all planned with such care would end in disaster.

By the time they were having lunch in a café in Victoria Street, Marion had worked so hard to improve the atmosphere that she was quite exhausted, and with very little to show for it.

Luckily, she spotted a number eleven bus, and made

a joke about how – except for the heat – they might just as well be back in Victoria Street in London!

This was taken up by Maggie, who announced that obviously the British only felt secure when *all* Victoria Streets in the whole wide world had number elevens lumbering through them. And then they all began to argue about which of the many things the British found most essential when they were cut off from home.

'Sash windows,' Alice shouted, the others topping her with 'digestive biscuits', 'proper breakfasts', 'whisky'; and even a still-sulking Dominica managed to murmur: 'undrinkable coffee!' This made them all laugh, and so Metro allowed herself the ghost of a smile.

In the end they enjoyed themselves so much and stayed so late that they were too exhausted to do anything but drift back to their rooms to rest, before changing for their grand reunion party at eight o'clock.

In the side ward of the surgery at the Centre where Kate was sleeping, she dressed quickly, for she was too preoccupied with Doctor Fraser's invitation to dinner to bother much with her appearance; so, as she had an hour to spare, she wandered into Bea's room and insisted on helping Bea with her makeup.

'Oh, very well,' Bea agreed ungraciously, producing a comb in which half the teeth were missing, and a box of Tolkon powder that was so white it made her look like a ghost. So Kate fetched her own, insisting on rouging Bea's cheeks and swearing that by the time she'd finished Bea would look fine and certainly *not* like a Dutch doll with a fever.

How cosy this is, thought Bea, and what a change to have a woman in the flat instead of just Stephen who didn't give a damn how she looked – *if* he noticed her at all.

'Kate, tell me something?'

'What's that?'

'Don't laugh, but have I got any hairs on my chin?'

'Good Lord, no.'

'It's my one dread. Only Stephen would never think to mention it – *when* he knows who I am. Half the time he thinks I'm Monica or Joss!'

'Talk of the devil,' Kate whispered, for Stephen had appeared in the doorway, and Beatrice could just make out that he was still wearing his so-called working clothes.

'Stephen! You're not going to Raffles like that I hope?'

'And why on earth not? I'll only be sitting in the bar with Jake.'

'Not in that pyja top you won't, and *you watch your drinking* while you're at it.'

With what could only be described as a flounce, Stephen shot out of the room, muttering to himself that he was not going to be bullied by a woman twenty years his junior, and if he wanted to have a skinful with Jake, then by God he most certainly would.

Jake was irritated. He was sitting at his desk trying to get through to the owner of a Rolls Royce, and the man's secretary was insisting that Sir John was *not* there, when Jake knew perfectly well that he was, because he could hear the man's voice growling away in he background.

Five years before, Jake had started a car-hire firm, buying up all the motor cars that had been requisitioned by the Army, and which hadn't been reclaimed because the owners were dead or were wanted for black market offences. He had done well, and anticipated doing even better if the trickle of tourists increased, and the Emergency didn't get even worse.

Impatiently, he dialled Sir John's other number, thinking that it was bad enough up-country, but now that the terrorists were moving into Singapore it was anyone's guess where it would end. This time he got through to Sir John's assistant, and managed to make an appointment for the next afternoon. Not that the car would be cheap, because the bastard was a diplomat and therefore public school, and they were the worst as he should know to his cost!

He stood up and stretched, slipping off his sweat-soaked clothes as he shouted to his man-servant to run a bath.

Damned public schools! When he thought of his own years at Marlborough, it was a wonder he'd even survived. Bad enough being a half-caste, without being sent to an establishment that was so devoutly Church of England, that when he hadn't been treated with patronising condescension, they were all set to convert him. Not that he hadn't been C. of E. from birth, but something perverse in his nature had made him insist that he was a Buddhist, and he'd stuck to it ever since. Bloody-minded even at that age, he thought, wondering if his dinner jacket was still presentable after the all-night party at Madame Evansky's.

He crossed to the drinks tray and poured himself a gin and bitters. Was he perhaps getting too old for this kind of shindig? The polite exchanges on arrival, the buffet with too much to drink, and then the slow disintegration as more and more couples slipped away, only to emerge an hour or so later for more drink and a mad drive home through the dawn.

He carried his drink and cigarettes into the bathroom, switching on the wireless so that he could enjoy his bath as he liked to: everything to hand and a good long soak to wash off the frustrations of the day.

'They asked me how I knew, my true love was true?
I of course replied, something here inside, cannot
  be denied.'

Damned silly crooner. The words were bad enough, but why did he have to sound as if he was about to be sick? Jake regarded his face in the shaving mirror that swung over the bath.

Given a few short years and he'd be indistinguishable from the rest of the band of middle-aged men who gathered at the Yacht Club to pick up any invitation that happened to be going. Hangers-on to the coattails of Empire, he thought, and all because the living was easy and how could a chap survive without servants? Not that *he* could manage it easily, for he'd lived in the East far too long. Had been born in it, come to that; and if he ever dreamed of England and his great-grandfather's house it was because he knew that with his record it was unobtainable. After all, apart from being expelled from school, his marriage to that rich drunken bitch hadn't helped. Come to think of it, that had been the last time he'd written to the old man, and then it had been to ask for money, so no wonder he hadn't even bothered to reply. Still, his black sheep grandson hadn't done so badly, all things considered.

Jake chucked the stub of his cigarette into the basin, and finished his drink. Twenty-two years old and Entertainments Officer on the P & O Line! He'd made a packet out of that, what with the kick-backs from the bands, and the women he'd wined and dined at their own expense. Not that he hadn't done even better when he'd jumped ship in Singapore, what with organising hunting parties up-country, and catching the new arrivals for the quick sale of a Cadillac, of which he was the sole Far East representative. Even the war hadn't been too much of a disaster, but then didn't he have a Swiss passport, and didn't the Japanese need an interpreter for the so-called neutrals?

He laughed out loud as he remembered the Japs' bewilderment because they couldn't understand the difference between the North and the South of Ireland; that Eire was neutral and that their civilians were demanding to be shipped home. Come to think of it, that had been one of his failures. He could still see Nurse Mary O'Brien screaming at a Commandant that she would report him to the Red Cross or even the League of Nations. At least he hadn't come to *her* sticky end.

Jake lifted the plug with his toe, lying in the bath and enjoying the air drying his body, before jumping up and padding out to his bedroom.

Damn! The bloody fan had stopped again – but then wasn't that the post-war East all over? Masses of new equipment arriving, without any of the locals having the ghost of an idea of how to install them. He buttoned his shirt before deftly knotting his tie and examining himself in the glass.

Still pretty presentable, he acknowledged, lifting his chin to pull the knot a shade higher, before sprinkling brilliantine on his hands and smoothing it over his hair.

'Lou,' he shouted to his man-servant, whom he could just see folding the *Straits Times* and adding it to a row of magazines.

'If anyone telephones and it's urgent, I'll be at Raffles. Tell them to ask for Bill the barman.' And with a quick check to see that he had enough money, he picked up his jacket and was gone.

Humour now quite restored, Dominica fastened the diamond clips to her dress, which she'd bought in Kuala Lumpur, paying far more than she could afford because she considered it money well spent – if only to be the most chic woman at the reunion. With some satisfaction she stared at her reflection, turning her body first this way and then that. Yes, she most certainly looked every inch a lady, and with a pat to her hair, she picked up her evening bag and made for the door.

By now the rest of the group would be safely downstairs so she could make her entrance alone, pausing perhaps on the stairs so that they would get the full glory of her toilette. Unfortunately, she ran into Alice and Marion chatting in the corridor, and more unfortunately still, they caught sight of her before she was able to slip back into her room. So with a charming smile she joined them, complimenting Alice on her dress, and noting that even Marion had taken some trouble with her appearance, and really looked quite elegant considering . . . Still, she didn't have *her* diamonds which, as she had explained to Teddy, so enhanced a woman of maturer years. It was with a sudden flood of affection for the woman who would never outshine her, that Dominica took Marion's arm.

'How very civilised this is, but if only dear Teddy were here. He *so* loves to see the ladies dressed up, though now we have this terrible Emergency, it's almost impossible to give a party!'

The strains of an Ivor Novello waltz greeted them as they descended the stairs, and when Dominica saw that Bea, Kate and Christina's dresses were hardly the height of fashion, she felt a quite overwhelming tenderness for her friends; so that when Kate remarked that they all looked gorgeous, she took it as a personal compliment, and graciously informed Stephen that she would do him the honour of sitting next to him. Even when the old fool turned to Bea and asked if he knew 'this female', she took it in good part, for the poor man was obviously gaga, and one must make allowances for those who were less fortunate than oneself.

Dominica glanced around the bar, smiling at everyone, and thinking that this was going to be a night to remember, and that dear Teddy would so enjoy the story of her triumph.

And then she saw them.

Alice had left to find Maggie and Dorothy because they didn't want to be late into the dining room, and it was Alice's shout that made Dominica glance towards the stairs.

'Dot! You look absolutely *marvellous* – and you too, Maggie.'

For a second Dominica thought she was going to faint as she took in the full glory of Dorothy's dress, which was dark blue lace and a flattering ballerina length. It was obviously a model, and possibly French, but what made her feel really ill was that Dorothy was wearing it as if to the manner born, and with that slight lift of the head which announced that she was very well aware that she was the best-dressed woman in Raffles – or possibly even in Singapore.

Dorothy was triumphant. She'd just show 'em, every

single one of them who at one time or another had put her down: Dominica for all the foul remarks she had made, and as for the others! Middle-class prigs, that's what they'd been, with their camp committees and always so set on doing the right thing. Until she was needed, that is. Then it was 'Get us some medicine from the guards. *Please*, Dorothy, you're the only one we can turn to.' It had never crossed any of their minds that they might have offered to go behind the huts themselves. Oh, dear me, no. After all, *they* weren't tarts. Whereas poor soiled Dorothy . . .

Just as she was about to join the others in the bar, Dorothy's eyes were caught by a lorry that was stopping in the driveway, and she thought how odd it was that the doorman had allowed the driver to block the entrance.

The next second she was running through the hall blind to everything: blind to Alice and Maggie as she pushed past them, blind to the guests she shoved so roughly aside, and blind to the porter whom she nearly knocked flying.

Oh, please, *please* let it not be a mistake.

And it wasn't. There, actually standing in front of her, was Sister Ulrica! With a cry of joy she threw herself into her dear friend's arms: a child who had lost her mother and suddenly and unexpectedly found her.

'So why didn't you let us *know*?' she shouted, relief making her sound angry as she examined Ulrica's face and re-set the eyes and the nose and the mouth that she'd found so difficult to recall when she thought she was dead.

'Didn't Marion and Bea get my letter?' Ulrica asked with surprise, holding Dorothy away from her and thanking God that she looked *so* well and happy. And Dorothy shook her head, beaming up at her old friend and demanding to know what she was doing driving a lorry for Pete's sake, and what's more simply covered in bullet holes!

Ulrica tucked Dorothy's arm into her own and they walked into the hotel, as incongruous a pair as they had always been: Ulrica in her white habit and cross, and Dorothy in her lace dress, her sheer stockings and hand-made shoes.

After Ulrica had greeted everyone and they'd re-covered from the shock of seeing her alive and well, and after she had been ushered into the dining room and agreed that, yes, it was a special occasion and, yes, she might allow herself a glass of champagne, she began to tell them something of her life during the past five years.

The leper colony where she had worked had been closed three years before, but instead of being sent to another colony or even back to Holland, she had been sent to a hospital deep in the jungle. Here, she had tended not only the sick but those injured in the skir-mishes of the Emergency; adding that they had treated both the victims and the Communists, for weren't they all God's children. Then she told them how she had joined the St Francis Xavier Service, because it gave succour *wherever* it was needed, and how she was now helping to settle the Chinese squatters in one of the new protected villages where, with God's help, they would be out of reach of terrorists.

Here Dominica butted in, explaining with the au-thority of one who lived up-country and knew what she was talking about, that the move was to stop the villagers being able to help the bandits with food and information.

'And to get them on our side,' Beatrice added enthusi-astically. 'If we're ever going to oust the Communists, it's the hearts and minds of the ordinary people we've got to win. Isn't that right, Christina?' And Christina agreed with equal enthusiasm, adding that at least the people would be given land of their own rather than working on somebody else's!

Always relating everything to herself, it occurred to Dominica that Christina might be getting at Teddy and his plantation, so that when Maggie remarked that it still couldn't be much fun to be uprooted without a by-your-leave, she hastened to point out that they too had known what it was to be deprived of *their* homes.

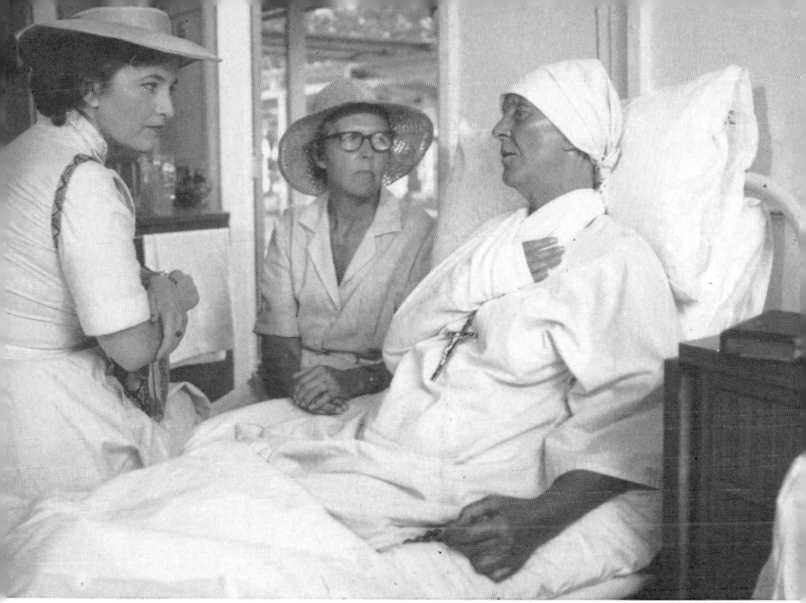

VERONICA ROBERTS as Dorothy, STEPHANIE COLE
as Beatrice, PATRICIA LAWRENCE as Ulrica

ELIZABETH CHAMBERS as Domenica, ANN BELL as Marion

CINDY SHELLEY as Alice, ELIZABETH MICKERY as Maggie,
VERONICA ROBERTS as Dorothy

DAMIEN THOMAS as Jake, VERONICA ROBERTS as Dorothy

EMILY BOLTON as Christina

PRESTON LOCKWOOD as Stephen,
STEPHANIE COLE as Beatrice

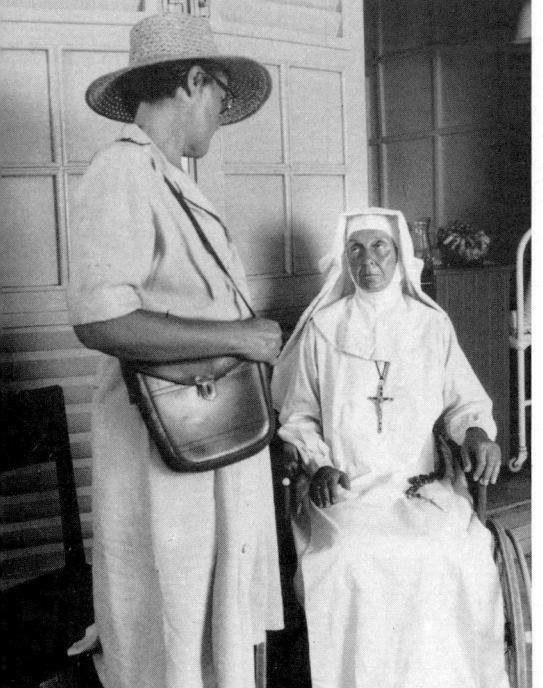

Above:
ELIZABETH MICKERY as Maggie, CLAIRE OBERMAN as Kate, VERONICA ROBERTS as Dorothy, DAMIEN THOMAS as Jake

Left: STEPHANIE COLE as Beatrice, PATRICIA LAWRENCE as Ulrica

PATRICIA LAWRENCE as Ulrica

DAMIEN THOMAS as Jake

All photographs copyright © BBC

'When *I* arrived at the camp, I had nothing but the rags I stood up in!'

'Rubbish. You had half your house with you,' Dorothy shouted at her, remembering how she had worked for Metro in order to earn a few dollars to buy food for little Violet. God Almighty, how she had *begged* for the job of doing her camp chores, while Metro had lain on her bed weakly protesting that she had one of her many headaches.

'Well, *you* didn't waste much time acquiring things from the guards, *did you*?' Dominica flashed back at Dorothy, for some reason feeling guilty and all the more angry because of it.

I might be back in the camps, Ulrica thought, glancing around the table, for however much her friends' appearances might have changed, their attitudes seemed to have remained exactly the same as when they had parted. Except for Christina, that is. She couldn't quite decide what it was, but it was something to do with Christina's expression which had once been so vulnerable, and now had a surety and determination that was most surprising. But then, hadn't Bea written to tell her how hard both she and Lau Peng worked, that they had a missionary zeal to educate, and that she didn't know what she would have done without them. Indeed, in the last letter, Bea had hinted that when she and Stephen did retire she had high hopes that the couple would take over, and that if they were married by then, they could even live above their work.

And now I can see why, thought Ulrica, for Christina looked so very capable, the type of woman who would be a rock in any crisis.

Ulrica sighed, thinking of how many crises they would still have to face in the poor, war-torn country, for that's what it was whatever the authorities chose to call it. And she should know!

No wonder Marion hadn't received her reply to her letter. Indeed, it had been a miracle that she'd still been alive to reply to it considering what happened.

She had been reading Marion's letter in her room at the Mission, and she remembered how excited she had been that there was a chance of seeing all her dear friends again. It was then that she had heard the first shots, followed by Father Joseph shouting the alarm, and she'd hurried outside to see what was going on, and if any help was needed. It was then that the explosions had begun as one grenade after another was lobbed into the compound, the last one so close that she had been thrown to the ground and had sprained her ankle.

She'd been lucky that time, just as she had been on the other two raids, but then the Good Lord had protected her, just as he had protected her from the Reverend Mother who had wanted to send her home because she was too independent. How unfathomable were the gifts of God, thought Ulrica, that this independence of mind had been returned to her after so long; that after a lifetime of obedience, it had been reborn with such a lusty cry in the barren wastes of her internment.

Sister Ulrica closed her eyes, praying to God that her stubbornness might also be used for His ends, and not for an old woman who, if she was honest, thoroughly enjoyed getting her own way. And then, being all too human, she justified her behaviour by telling God that her only wish was to help the good people of Malaya that she loved with such a deep and overwhelming passion.

'Wars . . . always wars,' Stephen muttered, glancing at Jake to check that he was ordering another drink from the barman. Dear, efficient Bill. How many years had he been mixing gin slings, and giving him the wink the moment he spotted Bea bearing down to take him home. Five, ten, twenty? Not that it mattered, because if it wasn't Bea it was Joss or Monica, or that fluffy little blonde who'd turned out to be such a tartar. Though not as bad as his sister, mind you; but then *she'd* turned down General Haig because she'd considered him rather too sloppy! Ah well, *plus ça change, plus c'est la même chose.*

'Seen a few wars in my time, dear boy,' Stephen announced, taking the drink from Jake and adding it to his glass. 'Fought in the 1914, don't y'know. Bit long in the tooth mind, but I managed to wangle it. Was even at Wipers.' And he toasted the battle and good old Freddie Lumsden with whom he'd shared a fox hole for almost two days. God, it felt almost like yesterday, and he still sometimes woke with that choking feeling and the heave in the pit of his stomach.

They'd been on a dawn raid into No Man's Land trying to bring back a rifleman splayed on the wire, his screams piercing the fumes of cordite until he'd been silenced for ever by a barrage of shelling. Only then had they decided to return, had almost made it to the trench when a shell ripped into their left flank and they had dived head first into a fox hole. Through the freezing dark of that night and the hell of the next day, they had lain there, the hole slowly filling with water which had turned into a sulphurous and muddy soup. And all the time Freddie had sung his favourite songs while the dark stain had seeped downwards to the hand with the fingers missing. *No.* Freddie would *not* have made it, but then neither had most of the others who'd swung along the roads of France as if they were on a picnic.

Stephen drained his glass and ordered the same again, though Jake suggested that perhaps it might not be wise.

'Bea's been on at you too, has she?' Stephen waved his glass at Bill, remarking that he bet the women were putting a few back as well!

Stephen was right. The women had ordered their third bottle of champagne. Even Ulrica was on to her second glass, and when Dorothy cautioned her that she might be arrested for being drunk in charge of a lorry, she smugly informed the table that she thought it prudent to stay at her old convent.

Marion, who'd been careful to limit her intake because

she knew that her friends would expect her to say a few words, decided to wait until after the meal, glancing round the Tiffin room as she rehearsed what she was going to say. It must be one of the most beautiful rooms in any hotel, she thought, glancing up to the balcony with its delicate traceries, and catching the eye of a couple who were looking down, their hands entwined and their heads close together. How many couples must have fallen in love in this room, and how many more had got engaged and run down the stairs to tell their parents? And did the couple up there realise all that had happened here during the war? She remembered how she had dropped in to say goodbye to a friend the day before she had left on the boat, and how extraordinary the place had seemed, what with the inhabitants living under siege, no staff and the only lighting from candles. In every corridor there had been lines of washing and mattresses on the floor, and over the whole hotel the heady smell of alcohol because the manager had been ordered to destroy the cellar. And now – it was as if that time had never been.

The band bridged smoothly into 'Let There Be Love', and Marion glanced back at the table and saw that everyone had finished their dessert, so she got to her feet and raised her glass.

'First I'd like to say how glad I am you could all be here tonight. It doesn't seem like five years, but then I suppose with real friends you just pick up where you left off. And I'm so glad that things have worked out for all of you: Dominica and Maggie both happily married; Dorothy a successful career woman; Beatrice and Christina doing such a splendid job at Joss's Centre; Ulrica fulfilled in her equally valuable work, and our Kate well on the way to becoming a doctor!'

Marion paused, sure that she had left someone out, so she asked them, and Alice piped up, shouting an embarrassed 'Only me and I haven't done anything except break off an engagement.' So Marion quickly reassured her that it was probably the right decision, and that there was no point in hanging on to something if it wasn't going to work out!

A hush fell over the table, each of the women aware that Marion's remark could equally refer to herself; and Marion, who was well aware of what they were thinking, hurried on.

'No doubt we'll have plenty of time to drink each other's health, so tonight let's remember all those who were in the camps: those who are still alive, and those who died in captivity or because of those years.'

Her friends looked away, anywhere except at each other, so that it was some seconds before anyone registered Marion's next proposal which was that they should remember not only their own, *but their captors as well*.

Suddenly, it was as if an electric charge had run through the table, dividing it into hostile camps: Ulrica and Christina agreeing with Marion, and the rest of them horrified that she'd even dared to make such a suggestion.

Beatrice was incensed, reminding them of all her patients who had died because of their captors, particularly Yamauchi who had denied them their parcels with the life-saving medicines. She was especially angry with Christina, who had chipped in that whatever he had done, Yamauchi had *not* been a monster; while Marion tried to stop them all, shouting that what had happened hadn't been half as simple as Bea was trying to make out. But the majority of the women were against her, calling out the names of those they had lost, in order to prove their point: Mrs Courtenay, Rose, Sally, Mrs Bowen, Debbie, Sylvia, and for God's sake – this from Beatrice – what about little Violet and eleven-year-old Susie?

The air seethed with the names of the dead, and the people at the other tables turned to stare as a now desperate Marion battled on, reminding them all that Yamauchi had paid for what he had done, for hadn't he been hanged, while so many of the others had gone free, and what's more, for far worse crimes.

'Yes,' Christina added with bitterness, 'including some of the Kempei Tei secret police, but then they were *much* too useful to the Allies to ever be hanged, let alone punished.'

Gratefully Marion turned to her, thinking that Christina was backing her up, and agreeing that if Yamauchi's trial hadn't been so early, he'd have probably been sent back to Japan like so many others. But Christina's face was hard as she retorted that that was only because the Prosecution had run out of money; that one day the criminals were in jail and the witnesses waiting to give evidence, and the next, they were roaming free in a city where they had murdered and maimed thousands. 'And what about the Americans?' she demanded. *They* had stolen criminals from under the noses of the British, shipping them out under cover and all because they had information about Chiang Kai-Shek and Communist China – information the Kempei Tei had prised from their prisoners under torture!

The party that had begun so splendidly, now disintegrated into an angry shambles, accusations and justifications flying across the table, as Marion and Ulrica pleaded for forgiveness and the rest of them refused to listen.

In the end Marion managed to win the day, but it was a hollow victory, for though they did drink to all those who were in the camps, Dominica, Dorothy and Maggie made it obvious that they were only paying a resentful lip service, while Bea was still so incensed that she flung at Marion that no doubt they'd be drinking to the Communists next!

'That went like a bomb,' Maggie remarked, turning to Dorothy for sympathy. But her chair was empty.

Dorothy had had enough.

Stephen had fallen asleep, his thin form humped like a camel, and a wisp of his hair rising and falling with his breath.

Alone in the bar, Jake was talking to Bill, an old ally since before the war, and whose information had made them both a packet of money.

'So, Bill, if you see him again just give me the nod.' Surreptitiously, Jake pushed a note across the bar, and it slipped into Bill's pocket as if drawn there by a magnet.

'I see you're bribing the barman again.'

Smoothly Jake turned and smiled, before standing and offering Dorothy his stool.

'Party over?'

'So far as I'm concerned.' Dorothy edged herself on to the padded top, arranging the skirt of her dress with a manicured hand. 'Jake, let me buy *you* a drink. After all, I owe you one.'

'Whatever for?' He noticed that she was wearing a scent he hadn't smelt since the war, when he'd slept with a girl from the Swiss Embassy who'd been very helpful over a currency deal.

Dorothy ordered a gin sling and a Tiger beer, before turning and giving Jake a broad grin and nudging him in the ribs. 'But for you I wouldn't be where I am! Remember when you took Maggie and me to find some furniture for my bungalow?'

'And you learnt to spot a Hepplewhite in one minute flat? By God, you were a scruffy little thing, but you certainly had guts.'

He picked up his beer and saluted her. 'Money suits you.'

'It suits everyone!' Dorothy replied. With which sentiment he could not but agree, thinking that Dorothy looked like a cat who had not only drunk the cream but knew where there was plenty more to be had.

'So, Jake. How do *you* make out these days?'

Here it comes, he thought, the questions he had been hoping wouldn't be asked; but with his usual aplomb he hinted at a sideline here and a deal fixed there, and *no* he did draw the line at opium, but anything else . . . And beyond that he would not be drawn.

'Dorothy, Maggie tells me you're on the lookout for some ivory?'

'Got any contacts?'

'I might have.'

'Then why don't we get together?'

And Dorothy smiled at him with such innocent eyes that he knew that it was deliberate, and he wondered if the rest of her was as appealing as her face.

After the breakup of the party, the women had fled from the dining room; not only to get away from each other, but from the curious gaze of the guests and the staff. The two allies, Marion and Ulrica, made for the garden where they could hide, for its darkness was broken only by the moonlight and the occasional candle.

The white uniform of the waiter appeared disembodied as it glided across the grass with a tray of coffee, the friends now enjoying an evening breeze that carried the smell of the sea and the faint hint of jasmine.

Here under the stars was something they understood: the timeless beauty of the East, its humid warmth lulling them back into a sense of well-being that had been so rudely shattered by the women they had thought they knew as well as themselves. And of course they did. That had been half their trouble, for in a way they had been arguing *with* themselves. For however tolerant Ulrica and Marion were, they had known what the reaction would be; and that it would make *them* entrench their position – if only in fear of their own dark anger, that somewhere in the depths of their being lay waiting to reclaim them.

Even now, in their exhaustion, they were not able to leave the subject alone, for they continued to discuss Yamauchi: how Ulrica had visited him to the end, and how he had welcomed death, not only because of his country's defeat, but because of the news that his daughter and grandson had been in Nagasaki when the atomic bomb had been dropped.

At last they fell silent, occasionally catching each other's eye and thanking God that they at least had each other for comfort.

Marion was the first to break the silence.

'I'm afraid I've upset Bea terribly, and I didn't mean to. You know how prickly she is about having volunteered to give evidence against Yamauchi; but if anyone's to blame for his death it was Clifford. He was gunning for him from the word go.'

And they lapsed into silence again, Marion remembering Clifford's distress because he had spent the war at a desk job in England, while his wife had been captured and made to suffer. No wonder he'd become obsessed with bringing Yamauchi to justice, if only to temper his guilt; but it was *she* who had made him feel guilty, and that hadn't been a help to either of them.

Ulrica seemed to read her thoughts, for she asked Marion what had happened between her and her husband? 'I had hoped things would have worked out, you were both trying *so* hard.'

'The effort was too much.'

Ulrica unfolded her hands and stared at them, thinking how very old they looked in the moonlight.

'A divorce cannot be easy.'

'No.'

Marion was on the point of unburdening herself about all the secret fears that she had never told anyone, when she spotted the solid form of Dominica tottering across the grass. As she came nearer, Marion saw that her eyes were shining and her hands clasped tightly together as if she was about to fall to her knees and pray.

'My dears, I've just had *the* most brilliant idea. Three weeks is far too long to spend in Singapore, so I've decided you must all come up-country and stay with me! *I insist*. And dear Teddy would love to meet you all, so what about the weekend after next?'

Marion and Ulrica were so surprised that they did not

reply immediately, so Dominica turned to Ulrica for support. 'You've been to stay, so *you* tell Marion how very pleasant it is.' But before Ulrica was able to do so, Dominica was rattling on again about the plantation and bungalow and her lovely garden, and how Cookie made such very delicious meals, and how she had *so* much space for entertaining, that it would be such a pity if . . .

It seemed she would never stop, and the two friends had some trouble in keeping a straight face, for they were reminded of all the many times Metro Goldwyn had interrupted other conversations; and Marion felt a sudden and extraordinary warmth for this silly woman, who was so like a child in her enthusiasms and petulance; and that maddening though she might be, she would not change a hair of her head.

At least, not many.

5
Singapore

The next morning, Ulrica rose at dawn, and after a hurried prayer, including one begging for strength for she was still exhausted, she climbed into the lorry and set off for the Mission.

However, Dominica's departure was somewhat delayed: not only by her repeated goodbyes to everyone except Dorothy, who had failed to appear, but by her constant reminders that – apart from Beatrice and Christina who said they couldn't leave the Centre – she would see them all in a week's time. It seemed to Marion, who was also very tired, that Metro would never stop twittering on about how she was *so* looking forward to their visit, and so was dear Teddy of course because she'd already rung him, and maybe she'd have a party and then they could all meet her good friend Lady Freda, and oh dear there was so much to arrange that really she couldn't think . . .

The friends' last sight of Metro was clambering into Teddy's armoured car, still talking non-stop to the driver and guard. 'And you must remember to stop at the delicatessen, and then there's Robinson's for they're sure to have something I need; and besides, the sight of so many pretty things always cheers me when I'm setting off into the unknown.'

When the driver reminded Dominica that he had been instructed to drive her straight to the plantation, she snapped back that as far as she was concerned, it *was* the unknown, for she certainly did not know any of the bandits who might be waiting to spring out and murder her for her jewels.

She was still chatting as the car drove away, and her friends, who had now been standing in the drive for what seemed like days, decided that they deserved a restorative cup of tea before going their separate ways: Marion, Maggie, Kate and Alice to look up old haunts, while Beatrice and Christina returned to their routine of work.

Not that there was anything routine about the pile of papers that confronted Beatrice after only a day's absence. 'If my title is Mole,' she told herself wryly, 'then it's a mole who's trying to move a bloody mountain!'

Continuing to mumble her displeasure, Beatrice sat down at her desk and tried hard to concentrate; but somehow the break from her work had disturbed her rhythm, and she stared at the 'In' tray with something akin to panic: for now that Christina and Lau Peng were working full-time in the school, the administration was becoming a never-ending nightmare. And as for Stephen! The old boy was a positive menace, if not downright dangerous – but then what else could she expect given his age and the state of his health?

Popping the last of the acid drops into her mouth, Beatrice opened the first letter, which was a reply to one of her own concerning the drains. *Hell and damnation!* She was being passed on to yet another department, which meant yet another letter and no doubt another damned silly reply! Well, if they didn't watch out they'd be up to their civil service necks in yet another outbreak of dysentry, what with the mounting unemployment, and her patients forced to buy food from hawkers who didn't give one jot about anything as mundane as hygiene – *if* they knew what it was, which she very much doubted.

Absentmindedly, Beatrice wiped the sweat off her spectacles, staring at the dim outline of the correspondence, and thinking that it just about summed up the whole bang shoot: a never-ending blurr!

'Only me,' Kate shouted, entering the office and filling it with her energy. 'Look, I've never been much of a one for sightseeing, so I wondered if you could do with some help?'

'Kate, don't be absurd. You're here for a well-earned rest, not to bury yourself in *this* stinking chaos.'

'But I want to help. I really mean it, in fact I insist and you know how stubborn I can be!'

'Don't I just.' Bea replaced her spectacles, peering up at Kate and thinking how reliable she looked and what a joy she would be to her patients once she'd got her M.D.

'*Please*,' Kate begged, leaning over the desk as if she might take the Centre by force if she didn't get her way that very instant. And because Bea was overworked, she allowed herself to be persuaded, taking Kate to the surgery and hardly needing to explain anything, before Kate was buckling to as if they'd been working together ever since their internment.

In the days that followed, Bea was happier than she'd been for a very long time, for she could talk to Kate about the patients' many problems, as she never could to Christina and Stephen.

As for Kate, she too was happy because she was needed and she knew how Bea liked things to be done, so that quite often they wouldn't speak for minutes on end as she anticipated what was wanted, or acted as Bea's eyes just as she'd done in the sick bays.

Every afternoon, Kate arrived sharp at two o'clock, and went through the out-patients' files for the day. Then she would report to the surgery, suggesting that she take over this or that task, and doing it with such cheerful efficiency that very often the local assistants would consult *her* instead of bothering the doctor. It was the perfect partnership, and when they went up to the flat for a break and a cup of coffee, Bea no longer felt drained as she had so often just lately.

Even Stephen seemed to draw strength from Kate's presence, though the way he nagged her to get Bea to go off to the house party so infuriated Bea that on one occasion she actually threw a plate at him. Not that Stephen minded, for he enjoyed nothing better than a good row in front of a witness. 'You see, Kate, this is how this hoyden treats me,' he shouted. 'And if you don't get her off my back up-country, I'll sneak to Duncan that you're an opium addict or worse!' But Bea was adamant, saying that there was much too much to do; and besides, if she turned her back for a second, he'd be drunk or stuffing his face with curry puffs, and then she'd be up all night holding his stupid head!

It was towards the end of the week, when they'd seen out the last of the patients and were taking a breather, that Bea told Kate exactly how bad her eyesight had become. 'It's no use pretending. I can't even see to examine the patients – have to have an assistant all the time. Oh, I can diagnose, prescribe and advise, but let's face it, I shall never be able to practise again.'

Kate thought she would burst into tears when Bea took off her spectacles and stared sightlessly into the future; and she felt even worse when Bea looked up and smiled with that special sweetness that had always transformed her.

'Kate, you don't know what it means to me, your carrying on the torch.'

And with those words, Kate's short-lived happiness was destroyed, though when Doctor Fraser telephoned and asked her to dine for the second time, she had to admit that she didn't feel *quite* so depressed.

Duncan had arranged that they would meet at the Orchid restaurant, which he said was typical of the many small restaurants in the Chinese quarter, and generally meant that the food was delicious and the décor was not.

Needing to be by herself for a time, Kate arrived early; and while she was waiting she tried to cheer herself up by reminding herself of the evening that she and Joss had dropped in at just such a restaurant, and how Joss had launched into one of her more splendid Indignations, when she had demanded to know how it was possible that a race that could produce such exquisite water colours, could at the same time tolerate décors of such unique ugliness. 'Hell's bells, they're either as clinical as a public lavatory,' she had barked, while at the same time beaming at the sheer beastliness of the place. 'Or, if they do go in for a bit of arty-tarty, it's red lanterns with fringes that tickle your head, and giving so little light that half the time you're trying to eat your napkin, which is also red, as are the walls and the blinds, and for all I know the waiter's underpants, and that's my *last word*.' Which of course meant that it never was, for like many good-natured people she loved nothing better than to attack, if only to keep up the front that she was tougher than the Japanese boots she'd always insisted on wearing, despite Mrs Bristow's kind offer of sensible lace-ups.

'Sorry, Kate. Am I very late?'

'On the contrary, Duncan. I got here early.'

'You're just being kind.' Duncan lightly touched Kate's shoulder before sitting opposite her, elbows on the table and a great grin on his face as he told Kate that she was a sight for sore eyes, and that if she didn't watch out he'd monopolise every spare minute of her time and that was a threat!

It wasn't until the meal was over, when they were drinking China tea in minute bowls, that Kate was able to voice the horror that she had felt when Beatrice had made her remark about carrying on the torch.

Duncan had been chatting about his work and how, apart from the hospital and his lectures, the three mornings a week at the Centre gave him more satisfaction than the rest of his jobs put together. Then, because it invariably made him uneasy to talk about himself, he turned the conversation to Kate's work, asking her what she thought of specialising in once she'd become a doctor?

She hadn't wanted to unburden herself, hadn't wanted to spoil a second of their evening together, but before she could stop herself she found that she was telling him how she was seriously thinking of chucking the whole thing in.

Duncan didn't look shocked or even very surprised, only asking Kate if it wasn't perhaps what they used to call mid-term-itis? But Kate was quite sure that it wasn't, that it was something to do with the endless restrictions and the remoteness of everything: that what really stuck in her craw was being lectured at by doctors who were sometimes the same age as she was, and what's more hadn't half her experience.

'I mean in camp, once Bea's sight had deteriorated, I did everything – but *everything*. Hell, I even amputated a leg, and there was no flaming text book to go by.'

Duncan nodded his understanding, picking up some salt that had spilt and throwing it over his shoulder: and it came to Kate that he'd been a doctor in Changi, and that she really had no need to explain anything because they'd both been through exactly the same experience.

'Kate, have you discussed it with Beatrice?'

'I've tried, but I can't. She's so darn proud of me, that I'd feel worse letting *her* down than my own family.'

'Now you listen to me, Nurse Norris,' Duncan instructed severely, grabbing her hands and holding them between his own. 'Our Beatrice is a tough old bird and she'll cope, honest to God. When I think of what she's achieved in the past few years and the knocks she's taken, and how she's picked herself up and gone straight on back into the fray. Take her blessed drains, for instance. You've only to whisper "Doctor Mason", and the entire Sewage Department cringes behind their desks. I promise you! Why last time round, she even stormed down to the Head of Department, and when she discovered he'd locked himself in his office, what did she do but swipe the key from another door and go storming in with all guns blazing. I'm told the row was such a

blistering corker that when she finally left, the poor
bugger took the rest of the day off!'

But though Kate laughed, and indeed, thoroughly
enjoyed the rest of the evening, somewhere inside her
was the dread that if she ever plucked up enough courage to tell Bea her decision, it would surely break her
heart.

Beatrice decided that it was one of those rare moments
in her life when she needed bucking up, so she plonked
herself down at the table of a café in Queen's Street and
daringly ordered a pink gin.

It wasn't as if she hadn't been entirely reasonable. Far
from it! After all, if a patient with T.B. didn't justify
rehousing, then who did? But then wasn't it always the
same since the civil service began – which come to think
of it must have been straight out of a Gorgon's head,
fully departmented and briefed on all the many ways of
obstructing one Doctor Mason. Huh! And if the blithering idiots thought she had the time to go through the
so-called proper channels – whatever *they* were – they
had another think coming! Fat chance of doing that when
she was already fully stretched at the Centre, not to
mention Stephen giving her incessant advice, and her
snapping the poor love's head off when she ought to be
nothing but sweetness and light.

The memory of his specialist's report pained her to
even think of it: heart on its last legs, blood pressure
over the moon, and as if that wasn't enough, a liver the
size of an egg. Not that she hadn't known for some
time, hadn't avoided knowing even while she watched
Stephen grow ever weaker. And the trouble was that if
she did try to be nicer to him, he would only smell a rat.
No. Better to go on as they had always gone on: bickering
and rowing, with the occasional moment when they saw
eye to eye and would wink at each other like two silly
chumps.

At last the waiter arrived with the drink, and Beatrice
knocked half of it back in one go. How long did the poor

boy have? If she was honest? A year perhaps – or even fourteen months if he didn't do anything rash, which knowing him was impossible. And then what? For by that time she would be almost blind, if not completely.

There was only one thing for it: tackle Christina and Lau Peng. After all, they were not only dedicated but more than capable, and if they did get married, which she bet her buttons they would, then what could be more convenient than a flat over their work?

Beatrice lent across to an empty table, and pinched a plate full of peanuts which someone had left. What a blessing it had been, that Lau Peng had turned up out of the blue like that, though why he had come to the Centre was anyone's guess. But then, the Chinese weren't called inscrutable for nothing, and the day she understood what made them tick, she'd probably be in her dotage. The important thing was that he was good at everything he did. Take the adult education classes. Honestly, sometimes it felt as if he was teaching every Chinese in the whole damned Colony. Why, only the other night when she'd been lying in bed and trying to sleep – must have been well past eleven – she could still hear him instructing some group or other. No, he and Christina would be the perfect pair to take over, and the sooner she let go of the reins the better for all concerned.

Having made up her mind for the hundredth time, Bea paid the bill and started her trek back to the Centre, walking steadily and always close to the walls so that she wouldn't bump into anyone, though her steps faltered as she reached the intersection with Middle Road.

Damn it, she didn't feel like going back, not one little bit. In fact what she felt like was a good old gossip with Marion and a cup of tea in the Tiffin Room. Having decided to play hooky, she quickened her pace, thinking she might go the whole hog and have one of those delicious cream buns with a dusting of sugar on the top.

She was within sight of the hazy but distinctive outline of Raffles, when a woman pushed past her almost knocking her down, and if it hadn't been for a 'So sorry' flung over the woman's shoulder, she would never have known it was Marion. What on earth's going on, Beatrice muttered to herself, straightening her specs, and trying to make out which way she was pointing. Honestly, it wasn't at all like Marion to behave like that, in fact something must most definitely be up.

For a moment, Beatrice deliberated if it might not be better to forgo her visit, but curiosity got the better of her; just as it had got the better of her when she'd planted sunflowers in the kindergarten window box and then dug them up to see how they were getting on.

Just as Marion had taken a bottle of gin out of the wardrobe and fetched a glass from the bathroom, there was a knock at her bedroom door. 'Who is it?' she shouted, her voice sharp and unwelcoming, and if it had been anyone but Beatrice, she would most certainly have sent them packing.

'Thought I'd look in to see if you fancied a cuppa,' Bea announced brightly, but Marion snapped back at her that she needed something a darn sight stronger than tea thank you very much, and before Beatrice had time to ask why, Marion was telling her.

For some reason she'd woken that morning with a longing to see her old house again, and after Metro had left, she'd set out with high hopes of enjoying herself. However, the reality had been very different. The moment she'd caught sight of the house she knew that she should never have come, for it had changed beyond all recognition. Gone was the tree she'd planted to celebrate a wedding anniversary, and gone were the flowers she'd grown for the house. In their place was a front garden edged with borders of almost military precision, a tarmac drive, and worst of all a garage where they'd once built a lily pond. If it was possible, the house was even more of a stranger, with a wrought-iron gate in front of the door, and on either side matching wrought-iron holders for hanging baskets, which were resplendent with every flower that man had managed to propagate in a colour not naturally its own.

At this point, Marion began to giggle, but Beatrice could see how the changes had thrown her, for the hand that picked up the glass was shaking and even her voice was none too steady.

'So, Bea, I decided to cheer myself by visiting the neighbours, a Mr and Mrs Flower, who had been old friends.'

After the briefest of pauses, the couple had invited Marion to join them in the garden, and it was then that their attitude had become only too apparent, for they had remarked that it was *so* nice that Marion could occupy her time in such a worthwhile job as the Red Cross Library; and how very lucky she was that Ben had got up to Oxford, but then they'd always known he had his father's brains! That had been bad enough, but when she'd asked them what they were doing that evening, having thought of inviting them both for drinks, they had hurriedly made the excuse that they would have *loved* her to join them, but unfortunately they were having a formal dinner, and she *must* know how imposs-ible it was to cope with uneven numbers.

'I tell you, Bea, it would've been a very different story if Clifford had called. Then it'd have been: "A new wife? I *say!*" Not to mention "Who could blame him for getting shot of that neurotic creature, so let's ask him to dinner!" It's all so bloody unfair.'

'Since when was life fair to a woman on her own?' Bea demanded, remembering the years of isolation when she'd worked in various hospitals, plus the fact that if she had sought companionship, she'd have been required to give in her resignation.

'At least, Bea, you've always been someone in your own right. Whereas, except in the camp, I've only ever been thought of as part of Clifford, and now it seems I have no identity at all!'

By this time Marion had worked herself into a rage, so Bea attempted to calm her by remarking that all recently divorced women probably felt the same, but Marion would have none of it. 'It's nearly two years,' she flung at her; and when Bea suggested that at least her work must be a comfort, Marion was quick to point out that however interesting the library might be, she still had to return to an empty house night after bloody night.

It was at this point that Bea sensed that there was something that Marion had left out, and which was fuelling not only her anger but her obvious distress. So she asked her, and with much difficulty Marion muttered that just before she'd left London, she'd received a letter from Clifford telling her that he and his wife were having a baby.

Ah, *now* I see it all, thought Bea, remembering Marion's visit to the Centre, and her look of longing when she'd caught sight of the little ones playing ring-a-ring-a-roses. And she stared at her friend's bent head, as it came to her how lonely Marion must be. After all, she'd always had someone to look after: first her husband, and then her son, and then the women in the camps. And now she had no one except a grown-up Ben.

'Bea, did I ever tell you that Clifford wanted *us* to have a baby? Around the time when things were starting to fall apart?'

Bea shook her head, thinking how typical of Clifford to see a new baby as the answer to everything: the patching up of their marriage, and with his newly independent wife tied to the house so that she'd have no chance of getting a part-time job. Poor honourable Marion, what agony she must have gone through having to say 'No' because it would be for all the wrong reasons.

Absent-mindedly, Beatrice reached for Marion's glass, wondering how she could comfort her, when if she was honest there was no comfort for something beyond recall.

'Marion, you still have Ben.'

Marion stood up, before changing her mind and sitting down again, and pushing her legs out and studying her feet as if they'd become objects of extraordinary interest.

'I'm just somewhere to dump his things!'

'Come now, I'm sure you're more than that,' Beatrice insisted, but Marion shook her head. And when Bea asked how she and Ben had got on after her return to England, Marion mumbled that Ben had been most painfully shy.

Bea could just imagine how it had been: Marion over-sensitive, and Ben at that awkward age when he was too self-conscious to show his feelings – especially to a mother who must have changed almost beyond recognition.

'Did you bridge the gap later?'

'Never had much of a chance, what with boarding school and conscription and then up to university.'

Marion heaved herself up and turned to the window, and Bea sensed that she was crying, so she filled the silence by talking about her father and how *she* hadn't managed to get any closer to him, even when he was dying.

She could see the scene as if it was yesterday: the blinds half drawn against the immoderate sun, so that the only light appeared to come from the sheets which were as starched and as crisp as a clergyman's collar. Just as her father had seemed starched, from the top of his thick white hair to the slim hands which had never done a day's work in their life, though he had always exhorted his flock to take pride in their manual labour. Oh no, he had died as he had lived: the 'perfect' stranger. And when, at the reading of his will, she had learnt that he had left his atheist daughter a brass cross, she had walked out of the room with the knowledge that she would never again return to the house that her sister called home.

Oh crumbs, now *I'm* going to blubber, thought Beatrice, and because she was cross with herself, she blamed her state on Marion, for as everyone knew she had never cared two hoots for that dreadful father.

'Bea, change your mind and come to Metro's.'

'Don't *you* start. Besides . . . I can't.'

'Is it your eyes?'

Oh heck, thought Bea. She's always been quick off the mark, especially where I'm concerned. So she decided that she might just as well come clean, and besides it would be a relief not to have to hedge for once.

'Just about. I can cope in familiar surroundings, but up there I'd be lost.'

'Not if *I'm* with you.' Marion leant forward, and Bea could just make out how enthusiastic she looked. '*Please*, Bea, if only for me. I mean, at least it'll show that I'm needed by someone.'

And because part of her wanted to go, and because Bea was nothing if not kind, she smiled at her friend and said yes.

If that Phyllis Bristow – she of the bloody R.A.P.W.I. – could only see us now, Maggie gloated, tucking her arm into Alice's as they browsed through the stalls of China Town looking for presents to take home.

Stupid old cow, she'd most likely have a seizure, her little innocent pet spending a whole day with that nasty common Maggie, who was nothing but a goodtime girl out to corrupt. Not that she was a goodtime girl now, being a respectable married woman and a mum to boot! While Alice had hardly changed a scrap, not since she'd been marched into their camp, all of fourteen, and hanging on to her Mum like grim death.

Crikey, when she thought of herself at that age! Or, let's face it, at twelve, when grim death had shoved *her* poor Mum under the sod, and left her to look after Dad and the tinies. Not that they hadn't made out. They'd been all right till those authorities poked their noses in, and all because the head teacher had started to suspect she were preggers.

Even now the terror of when they'd interrogated and got her to blow the gaff was too awful to even look at except sort-of sideways. Poor, lonely Dad. All he'd ever done was take a bit of comfort from her, and let's face it, it hadn't been difficult what with them all sharing the same bed. And out of that . . . Dad locked up, and them social workers shoving the tinies out to those homes, and her landing up in the hospital miscarrying all over Out Patients. That was when she'd overheard someone whispering it were because of Dad topping himself that she'd lost it, and all things considered it was really for the best! So what was bloody best about slogging your guts out in Crossley Mill, with no baby and no Dad and no family, and all the time knowing everything's all your fault? No wonder she'd gone to the bad when she'd come out East with that Maisie Bradshaw. And up yours, Mrs Bristow of R.A.P.W.I.!

Maggie glanced across at Alice, who was playing with a Chinese puzzle, and again she marvelled that anyone could look so pure.

'Untouched by human hand', as they said on the sausages. Not that the camp hadn't left its mark what with Alice not remembering, and then breaking off that engagement. Mind, she must know something's up, or why else suddenly announce to all and sundry that she couldn't feel a thing since the day her Mum'd passed over in sick bay.

'Look, Maggie!'

Alice held up a rag doll in an Indian sari. 'Wouldn't she be just perfect for your Blanche?'

Maggie touched the tiny embroidered face, thanking God she'd had the guts not to get rid of little Blanche – even though she *was* a bastard and her Mum hardly remembering her soldier Daddy. Mind, she did have a faint picture of him kissing her in the back of that lorry, and shouting that she was the very first girl he'd made love to since he'd been captured. And by heck, that'd been some bunk up – that much she *did* remember, so small wonder she'd fallen for little Blanche.

Maggie relaxed and smiled as she thought of her daughter, and what a funny little scrap she'd been when they'd put her into her arms. It'd been the best moment of her life, that had, the warm bundle soft against her shoulder, and the tiny hand curling against the shawl she'd picked up on a barrow outside Dot's junk shop.

'I'll take the doll and the coloured ball,' Maggie told the trader, shoving the presents into her basket, as she checked that the camera she'd borrowed from Dorothy was still slung over her shoulder. Wouldn't do to have *that* nicked, not when she was much too beholden anyway.

'Come on, Alice, I'll take a snap of you. Stand over there by the arch.'

Alice turned to do so, and then stopped and pointed across the street. 'Look, Maggie! Isn't that Lau Peng? You *know*, Christina's boy friend from the Centre.'

'Where?'

'In front of the street library. Over there, talking to that Chinaman with the torn sleeve.'

'Oh yea. Hang on, I'll get a snap before he sees us and starts to pose.'

Maggie focused on Lau Peng just as he was handing a book to the Chinaman, and she thought what a good snap it'd be to show Jim: a typical slice of the East, what with the crowds and the stalls, and the library on wheels – which, come to think of it, would be a good idea for their district, with so many not feeling comfortable in the proper one.

After taking a quick snap of Lau Peng and then Alice, Maggie replaced the camera in its leather case, before shouting to Lau Peng to come on over and join them.

'Hallo,' he called, weaving between the traffic. 'It's Maggie, isn't it? And you're Alice! So how are you enjoying your stay?' And they told him very much, his smile growing even wider when he announced that he had persuaded Christina that he really could be trusted to look after the Centre, so she'd be coming up to Johore after all.

'Well done,' Maggie congratulated him, thinking how very efficient he looked, and so neat and clean that he made her feel an absolute shambles; and she suddenly realised how hot and tired she felt, and that what she longed for more than anything in the world was an early night, instead of having to cross town to meet Dorothy as they'd arranged.

Maggie was angry. It was past midnight, and she lay on her bed seething as she tried to finish her postcards to the family. How dare Dorothy stand her up without a by-your-leave, when she'd dragged herself half across Singapore so as to save the fare on a trishaw.

She poured herself a drink, listening to a girl laughing from the garden below. Must have been the one she'd passed coming up, she brooded. The girl with the perfect skin and three rows of pearls, who'd been grinning away at the officer. And that just about sums the place up, she told herself: a hotel for officers only, plus their ever-so-nice girlfriends who'd been to ever-so-nice schools and whose Daddies gave them allowances because they'd never have to soil *their* poor little pampered hands.

'Small wonder I'm a Socialist,' she informed the bottom of her glass, catching the faint sound of footsteps approaching, and then the door of the suite opening and banging closed.

'Right, Miss Moneybags, you're bloody well for it,' Maggie muttered. 'I've just about had it up to here, playing lady-in-waiting to your Lady Bountiful.'

Dorothy pushed back the curtain between the sitting room and the bedroom, throwing Maggie a casual hallo, as she kicked off her shoes and made for the dressing room.

'*And about time too!*'

'What's that supposed to mean?' Dorothy turned, looking not at all put out.

'What it *means*, is that we were going to the "Worlds", remember?'

'Oh, Lor! Sorry, Maggie. Only Jake and I went off to see *The Third Man*.'

'And sod me and my evening!' Maggie shouted, scattering her postcards and then stepping on them as she jumped off the bed. 'But then that's my role, isn't it? I mean, what I'm paid for? To hang about for your convenience and get lost when something better crops up. Jesus! When I think that I'd hoped it'd be like the old days with us mucking in, when of course you're now one of them, who thinks they can buy *anything* and *anybody*.'

Hands on her hips, Dorothy regarded Maggie with the same blank expression that she'd had in the camps whenever she'd been cornered.

'Well, if that's how you feel, you won't mind going up-country without me. *Will you*, Maggie?'

'*No, Dorothy, I bloody well won't.*' And Maggie ran into the bathroom, shouting back that she was looking forward to the good fresh air of Malaya, which didn't cost a penny and what's more didn't expect anything in return!

At the beginning of the week, Dorothy and Jake had been like two animals together: asserting themselves, while at the same time testing each other's weight.

First they had congratulated each other on how the years had passed over them so lightly; in fact given them some distinction and wasn't it nice to be them! Then they had moved on to their careers, though Jake had refused to go into detail about anything except his car-hire firm, only hinting that he was a middleman for a number of enterprises, and that in some ways the Emergency had been a positive bonus.

Knowing Jake, Dorothy had put the evasiveness down to him still dealing in illicit goods, and though he had protested that his black marketeering days were over, she was sure that he wouldn't have given up smuggling – if only in currency and gold. As for Dorothy, she had recounted every glowing detail of her rise to prosperity: the first shop where she and a pregnant Maggie had flogged their guts out; then, when Maggie had left with the baby to marry Jim, her move to the wrong end of Kensington, and the breakthrough when she'd discovered that the whole country was peppered with retired colonials only too happy to part with the mementoes they'd picked up when living abroad.

'It's like this,' she'd confided in Jake as they sat on the terrace of the Sea View Hotel. 'They're all feeling the pinch what with the cost of living and having to get by on a pension, so they're damned grateful for any spare cash they can lay their hands on. Anyway, I got this van for fifty quid, and took it all over the country picking up loads of stuff for an absolute pittance. And that's how I managed to get my present place in Church Street!'

She had felt so triumphant that Jake had felt a need to assert himself, and he had suggested that he took Dorothy to his contacts in the ivory trade, for she would be sure to be impressed by the reverence with which he was treated by the shopkeepers.

However, it hadn't worked out like that. At the very first shop, the owner had produced what appeared to be some very impressive pieces, only for Dorothy to declare that they were all a fake, and that the so-called eighteenth-century markings had been mocked-up with a dentist's drill. At which, instead of being insulted, the man had gone to a cupboard at the back of the shop, and produced genuine eighteenth-century erotica, treating Dorothy with a reverence he had never afforded Jake, though she had been so pleased with her purchases that she had taken him out to lunch.

It was over their pre-luncheon drinks that their defences had finally started to crack. Jake had enquired if Dorothy had any boyfriends in London, and Dorothy had found herself telling him not only about Alex and how he was married, but how she felt about the whole business of love and sex; that she'd always been happy to settle for sex with someone she liked, because falling in love inevitably ended by tying you down; and Jake had casually agreed, even toasting her for her guts. And it crossed Dorothy's mind how very unshockable he was, which must be the reason why she had always got on with him. That, and liking his looks.

Dorothy had then turned the conversation to Jake, asking about the rich widow he had always said he would marry; but he had shaken his head, saying that he was very choosy and still on the lookout. 'Not that I go without,' he had added quickly, hooking his finger into hers. 'I get by. Tell me, do you remember a Madam Evansky?'

'Not the Russian who ran the night club?'

'No, her friend. The one covered with diamonds. Anyway, she gives some rather amusing parties, and what with the planters' wives down for a break, and the girls at the cricket club, life can be pretty damned full.'

'I bet,' Dorothy had reassured him with a smile, and they found themselves laughing at how silly other people were because they didn't know how to enjoy themselves; and wasn't it nice to be on the same wavelength and not to give one tuppenny damn about what the world thought?

For the rest of the day they had drifted around Singapore, ending up at Raffles and dancing until the small hours, when they had gone on to a nightclub and had only separated when it finally closed at dawn.

After that, they had managed to meet every day, each of them secretly asking themselves why they hadn't made love, but hanging on to the moment because – though neither of them would ever have admitted it – the reality had so often let them down.

On the day before they had met for tea at the Sea View Hotel, and Jake had suggested that they went to *The Third Man*, because one or two people had been calling him Harry Lime, and that was the hero's name.

So they went.

This is absurd, Dorothy had told herself, sitting in the back row of a flea pit backing on to Raffles. I haven't done this since Dennis and I were courting. And the word 'courting', which was a word she would never have used out loud, carried her back to her childhood, when the world had seemed so very safe, and before it had ever occurred to her that there might be more to life than to marry and have some kids. Christ, but she'd been an innocent, and what's more had gone on being innocent, right through their engagement and the shy fumbles of their Brighton honeymoon. Even during her first adventure when they'd set sail for Singapore, she had still believed in the crock at the end of the rainbow.

How impressed she'd been by Dennis's job as a buyer at Robinson's, and the bungalow he had already bought, and where she'd imagined she would live for the rest of his working life. And then, two years later when little Violet had been born, how proud she had been of Dennis, that he'd given up his cricket so that he could spend his evenings decorating the nursery, because he didn't trust the natives to do anything really properly.

For the first time in her life, it had struck Dorothy how reactionary Dennis must have been; but then so had her mother, even muttering that Hitler was right about the Jews, and why should they be allowed to come to England and take jobs from their own unemployed.

She had glanced sideways at Jake, whose face in the flickering light of the film looked even more Indian than usual, and she thought how shocked Dennis and her mother would have been that she'd gone with Japs for a few grains of rice. But then, what did it matter, when her mother had been killed in the bombing, and poor Dennis had been shot by the Japs, and her little Violet . . .

It was some seconds before Dorothy had noticed the tears streaming down her face, and when Jake had passed her a handkerchief without asking why, she felt a surge of warmth that she wouldn't have believed possible. What a good and loyal friend he had been, even standing by her when that bitch had accused her of being a whore, and R.A.P.W.I. had shot her back to London. Why, he'd even driven her to the plane that

that Mrs Bristow had fixed up double-quick, 'Because we don't want a scandal now, do we?'

How many friends, let alone men, would have done *that*, Dorothy had asked herself; slipping her hand into Jake's, and noticing how dry his palm felt, even though the cinema was as humid as the hothouse at Kew.

Afterwards, they had drifted back to Raffles and sat in the garden drinking Irish coffee; not talking about anything in particular, but just enjoying each other's company; and it was then, for the second time, that Jake had asked Dorothy if she was really planning *not* to go up-country?

'What do you think?' she had replied, and he had stood up and said 'Thank you and goodnight,' because he was the only man she had ever met who knew when to leave her and when to stay.

6
To Malaya

Early the next day, two armoured cars complete with drivers and guards arrived in the forecourt of Raffles to pick up Marion, Maggie, Kate, Alice, Beatrice and Christina.

Beatrice had been amazed that Christina had suddenly agreed to come with them, if only that she was always so obsessive about her work and even hated to desert her pupils for half a day. Still, she could only suppose it was because of seeing her friends, and for once allowing herself to have some fun. As for Dorothy! It hadn't surprised her one bit that she cried off at the last minute, though she might have taken the trouble to tell them in person, instead of sending a message.

Beatrice settled herself in the back of the car, thinking what a change it would be to sit doing nothing more strenuous than chatting and enjoying the passing scene.

The morning was very misty, the streets almost empty except for the odd trishaw and car, and the industrious traders piling their stalls with bananas, pineapples, limes, oranges, vegetables and flowers.

This is the time I like best, thought Beatrice, searching her pockets for her barley sugars because a car journey always made her feel sick.

Marion too was thinking that the haze made the city even more beautiful, and how difficult it was to believe there was a war on; and yet only that morning she'd read of a warehouse being burnt to the ground, and that it was unlikely that there'd be any witnesses because of intimidation. Of course *that* she had gathered already, because of an incident the day after they'd arrived, when a terrorist had murdered a man just for giving evidence to the police, and then mown down his wife and children as an example to others. This, thought Marion, as they sped along Basah Road, is war at its worst, because the enemy could be anyone: the gardener in the N.C.O. club they were passing, the woman crossing the street, or even the cook in your own kitchen.

As the mist thinned out, so did the houses, for they were passing through the suburbs behind a convoy of soldiers singing 'Roll Out The Barrel' and shouting cheeky remarks at any car that dared to overtake them.

In a very short time they'd arrived at the frontier, which was all military efficiency, with a great deal of saluting and banging of boots, as a flint-faced sergeant searched the cars, his corporal pulling the luggage out of the boots, before shoving it back with such energy that Beatrice was driven to exclaim that he was *not* shoving shells into his cannon, and would he please mind what he was about!

It was over an hour before they were allowed to cross into Malaya, and it struck Beatrice – as it had done so many times before – that they were now travelling back in time to the days of the first settlers, for even on the road she could feel the hot breath of the jungle waiting to engulf them.

It leapt off the tarmac in humid waves, so that the landscape dipped and shimmered; and as the sweat coursed down her face, it was as if a great wet tongue had reached out to lick her. And there was something else: a kind of secrecy, as if the landscape was whispering under its breath. It was something to do with the way men stopped and stared as they passed; or a child would run into the dark mouth of a hut, the hand of a woman appearing for a second as it unlooped and dropped a curtain of sacking.

Then, suddenly, they accelerated round a corner and

plunged into the belly of the dragon. One moment they were passing through bright sunlight, and the next they were travelling through an underworld of shade enclosed by a roof of impenetrable green, supported by trunks covered with lichen and flowers and bright tendrils that twisted like ringlets over the branches; while the trapped air was engorged with the roar of the engines as they echoed back from the undergrowth or grew mute as they passed through a clearing. And all the time, insects and butterflies rose out of the clusters of flowers, before settling almost sleepily in their wake.

I'd forgotten, thought Marion. Not how beautiful the jungle is, but how alien, and she turned to watch the tracks of the car as if to reassure herself that there was still a way back to the city. You're just being morbid, she told herself, knocking a mosquito from the side of her neck. Think of all the times you were marched into the jungle to cut trees; and what about the trek to Camp Two, when they had walked for days living off what they could scavenge and sleeping where they fell? Whereas now, *now* they could all look forward to regular meals, proper beds, and for the first time ever, guards who were actually on their side!

They drove for the best part of a day, the jungle assuming a sameness that was broken only by burnt-out cars or patrols of soldiers, some of them camouflaged and weighed down with guns and grenades; but the only time the drivers agreed to stop was when they needed to go to the lavatory or for a security check by policemen with truncheons.

At the final road block, a Chinaman was being interrogated, a policeman holding him while another searched, his thin brown hands skimming the man's body before turning to his bicycle and ripping open the tyres, from whose centre illicit rice spilt, and damned the owner to death.

'I don't believe it,' Alice whispered to Maggie. 'He took that risk for just a few grains of rice?'

'That's him for the chop!' Maggie announced savagely,

though Beatrice was quick to point out that as he was helping the enemy, he deserved everything that was coming to him.

Nobody deserves that, thought Maggie. The poor bugger hadn't any choice, not with families tortured and then killed if they didn't collaborate. And into her mind came a picture of little Harry and Blanche waving good-bye, and she longed for them more at that moment than at any time during the holiday, wondering again if she'd been right to come up-country when there was always the risk of something nasty happening. She turned and stared out of the back window, wondering how much longer the jungle would go on, and deciding that how-ever much she hated the mean little street where she lived, at least she was surrounded by mates and knew where she was.

Finally, an hour later, they arrived at the fortified entrance to Dominica's plantation, where a board announced:

'The Sungei Kuching Estate.
Agent: Harrison and Derby
Manager: E. V. Forster-Brown.'

The friends were so tired that the plantation road seemed to go on for ever; until, about a hundred yards short of a garden glimpsed through the trees, they passed through a sinister barbed-wire fence. This time it was Alice who turned to stare back, her arms suddenly clasping her body as if she was trying to hold herself together.

Then they were out into the sunlight and an impec-cable lawn which sloped up to a large and beautiful bungalow, from the verandah of which, Dominica was waving frantically.

'Teddy! Teddy! At last my friends have arrived!' she shouted, hurrying down the steps, and closely followed by a houseboy who ran to unstrap the luggage.

'My dears! Didn't I tell you you'd be safe in our drivers' hands?'

The women clambered out of the cars, an ungainly group easing their limbs as Dominica fluttered around them and shouted for Teddy to come quickly and meet her dear, dear friends.

To Marion, Dominica's husband looked the archetype planter, sporting an open-necked shirt, baggy knee-length shorts, long thick socks, and heavy serviceable shoes. From his face, which was wreathed in a beaming smile, Marion guessed that he was around fifty, and by the look of pride that he threw his wife, she saw that he was as in love with Dominica as she was in love with him.

'Ah, the rest of the gallant band! Welcome to Sungei Kuching,' he boomed, and when he shook each of them by the hand, his grip was as reassuring as it was hearty.

He was particularly pleased to see Beatrice, solicitously asking her how the Centre was going, before turning to the rest of the group and confessing that he felt that he knew them already, because dear Dodo had told him so much.

'Dodo!' Maggie breathed with delight, desperately trying not to giggle, if only for Teddy's sake.

'So, Maggie? And where is Dorothy?' Dominica asked, well aware of what Maggie was thinking, and telling herself she was above noticing such very common behaviour.

'Fraid she had to call off, Dodo. Business reasons.'

'What a shame,' Dominica muttered, obviously not thinking that at all, and adding that *dear* Sister Ulrica was driving down first thing in the morning, and why didn't they all go inside where they could have some refreshments?

Amid much exclaiming and compliments, the friends walked up to the bungalow; Marion and Beatrice holding back so that no one would notice Marion counting the steps as she held Beatrice's elbow, guiding her towards a waiting Teddy who was carefully looking the other way. He knows about Bea's sight, Marion thought, grateful for the way he pretended suddenly to notice them only once they had gained the verandah.

'Can't thank you enough for coming,' he told them enthusiastically, lifting a chair to clear the way to the front door. 'Means the world to my Dodo. She gets very lonely stuck up here. Not that she doesn't put a brave face on it for my sake. But then, I hardly need to tell *you* what a plucky little thing she is.'

I don't believe it, thought Marion; and then into her mind flashed the picture of Metro juggling at the Camp's Christmas party, her swollen legs covered by a piece of cloth and her mouth tight with the pain of beriberi.

'Yes, she is plucky,' Marion replied with a smile, and the gratitude on Teddy's face told her that he knew perfectly well that his wife was more often a coward but that he simply didn't care; and Marion remembered Major Jackson who had also appeared an old duffer, but whose dignity when he had said his goodbyes to Metro had betrayed a depth of feeling not given to those who are truly stupid.

'I suppose you've noticed,' remarked Beatrice as they entered the bungalow, 'that it's a sight bigger than my Centre!' Her eyes scanned the vast polished floors and high ceilings as if she was measuring it for size and might, at any moment, open it as a squatters' rest home; while Maggie was fitting the whole of her house into the drawing room, thinking what fun Blanche would have had sliding up and down, and how easy her life would be with only one of Metro's army of servants.

'Of course, the place is smaller than my house on the island,' Dominica was quick to tell them. 'But *I* prefer this, it is much more of a home.'

'Even with all these guns?' Maggie called from the hall, where she and Christina were examining a rack by the door.

'But of course,' Dominica announced with pride. 'An Englishman's home is a fortress now, so that he can protect his Loved Ones! And not only that. Dear Teddy also has a secret store *and* with a great deal of ammunition. So you see, as I've already told you, you'll be quite safe here!'

A small Chinese woman entered from a passage leading to the back of the bungalow, and Dominica threw her a smile that was quite unlike the toffee-nosed Metro they thought that they knew so well. 'And here is Ah Chan, my amah. I really don't know what I would do without her and Cookie. But then we are *so* lucky with our servants, and they have been with Teddy for simply years.'

'If she goes on like this, I shall be sick,' Maggie whispered to Beatrice, who said yes it was a bit much, and that the sooner Metro reverted to her old grumbling self, the easier she'd be. This was partly because it made her think of herself and Stephen, and she wondered yet again if she shouldn't try to be nicer, despite the suspicion it might arouse. If only she wasn't such a devout atheist she could pretend suddenly to See The Light, but as it was, she was being trapped by her own nature and was now being punished for its lack of patience.

After more 'How wonderfuls' and 'Gosh, Dominica, you are lucky to have such a place,' the friends were shown to their rooms; Beatrice and Marion sleeping in the largest of the three guest rooms, which to Beatrice appeared to be very large indeed.

'Honestly, you could shove two of my offices into this, and still have the room to Rumba,' she announced as she sank on the bed, which instead of being hard like her own, gave under her so that she thought she was falling and clutched on to the side.

'If my mother were here, she'd have pronounced it "Very well appointed", and *she* hardly approved of anything except for Father and the Rochdale Town Hall.'

'And isn't Teddy simply gorgeous the way he looks at Metro as if she's the Bee's Knees?'

'Talk about rose-coloured spectacles! And doesn't he remind you of Major Jackson? The first time I clapped eyes I could hardly credit it. But then I suppose Metro's just the kind of helpless idiot who'd appeal to that sort of type. Still, jolly good luck to her, I say, considering her first was such an out-and-out stinker.' Bea leant forward, just as she had when she was dishing the dirt on the black marketeer in Camp Two. 'They do say his death was something of a mystery!'

'Oh Bea, do tell?'

'Weeeell . . . apparently he drove out one night and his car ran slap bang into a tree that'd conveniently fallen across the drive. Only thing was, the break in the trunk appeared to be very clean. You know, almost as if it had been chopped!'

'Golly! Can't have been much fun for poor old Metro.'

'On the contrary, from all accounts she was over the moon – not that she didn't smile bravely through her tears – you know how she is. And they do say he left quite a packet, hence the sparklers, which she likes to pretend were given by the Ever-Loving, whom I might tell you, I've a great deal of time for.'

'I must say she did look a bit like a Christmas tree – at the party, I mean. Oh Bea, isn't it fun to have such a good natter together?'

The friends grinned at each other, thinking how wicked they were and how very much they were going to enjoy themselves.

After dinner, which was five courses and seemed to go on for ever – Kate forced to undo her zip, and Bea wondering if she looked as purple as she felt – Teddy suggested that they gathered round the piano and had a go at his favourite Gilbert and Sullivan, because a little bird'd told him that Bea was something of a wizz on the ivories. Amidst cries of 'Come on, Bea', she shyly agreed to accompany them, just so long as she could telephone the Centre and check that everything was tickety-boo with Stephen.

'Treat the place as your own,' Teddy informed them all, his expansiveness showing itself in his gestures which had become more and more pronounced, ever since he had acted as barman, when he had informed the friends that he had a mean way with a cocktail!

Christina reminded Beatrice that the telephone was in the hall, and they went out together, Christina offering to get through to the exchange because she knew how Beatrice hated being made to hold on. And indeed there was a long delay, partly because of sabotage to the line, and when at last they did get through, Stephen was stuck in the lavatory. 'Typical,' muttered Beatrice, though Lau Peng assured her that everything was under control and yes, Stephen was taking his pills; so Beatrice passed the receiver to Christina, who immediately rattled away in Chinese, Beatrice thinking how authoritative she sounded in a foreign language, and not at all like a girlfriend but as if she was instructing one of her pupils. But then, as far as she was concerned, their whole relationship was a mystery, for they behaved more like an old married couple than two people in love.

Which just goes to show what a silly old softie I'm becoming, she told herself severely, remembering her mother who'd grown sickly sweet in her old age, and would yatter on for hours about all the good times they'd had when her daughters were young. Good times, my foot! There'd hardly been a day which *she* would have called good, and certainly not with a mother who never noticed anyone except her husband, for whom she'd been the perfect little helpmate, blast her cotton socks. And now, so it appears, I'm becoming just as sentimental, seethed Beatrice, stamping back into the drawing room and nearly falling over a chair. However, Marion caused a diversion by reminding Teddy that he'd promised to start off with a sing song, by way of limbering up to the full glory of an operetta.

'Ready to man the old Joanna?' he bellowed at Beatrice, rubbing his hands at the thought of the fun they were going to have, and pom-pomming a few bars as he adjusted the piano stool, though Beatrice had assured him that there was absolutely no need at all.

For the rest of the evening they sang their heads off. All, that is, except Christina, who sat and pretended to listen, or so it seemed to Kate, for she had that miles-away look in her eyes and was probably worrying about her pupils and how they were getting on with the assistant teacher.

When they had exhausted their repertoire of Gilbert and Sullivan, Maggie suggested that they sang some of the songs they'd sung in camp, 'Lilly of Laguna', 'Pack Up Your Troubles in Your Old Kit Bag', and 'Who's Taking You Home Tonight', so they did. And then Metro, who had sampled one or two of Teddy's cocktails in order to show how good they were, sang a lullaby in Dutch which she announced had been a particular favourite of her nanny's who had once worked for an Italian count! It was a particularly long lullaby, made even longer because Dominica couldn't *quite* remember the words, and insisted on going back to the beginning every time she faltered; and this, despite everyone assuring her that as they didn't know Dutch it didn't matter *what* she was singing.

Not that this stopped Metro, who continued in full and glorious flood.

It was during the fifth verse that Teddy whispered to Marion that he'd like to have a word with her, leading the way to the verandah as if he didn't wish to be overheard.

As they stepped into the cool of the evening, Marion noticed that Teddy's smile suddenly dropped, his eyes darting here and there as he stared into the darkness; and for the first time she understood what a strain it was, to be responsible for such a large area and the people who worked there; and she felt a wave of kindred sympathy, for hadn't she too been responsible for *her* group when she'd been their leader. The times she'd watched her friends being marched out into the jungle, and the fears *she'd* had that one day they might not come back.

'I wanted a word with you in confidence,' Teddy began, pulling away a creeper that had wound itself round a post, only to rewind it around his index finger instead. 'It's to do with Dodo – her future – should some bandits take a pot shot at me. It's always on the cards when I'm travelling out station. Thing is, she hasn't anyone but me. No people of her own in Holland, and she doesn't know my cousins in England – scarcely know 'em myself.' He suddenly focused on what he was doing, thoughtfully regarding the stem before chucking it away as if it was lethal. 'Marion, I'd feel so much easier if I knew she had someone to turn to.'

'Of course, Teddy.'

'I know how highly she regards you.'

'I'd do anything I could,' Marion assured him, trying to catch his eye to show that she meant it, but failing because he lowered his head as if in some way he was ashamed.

'I know what you're thinking, Marion. You're thinking why don't I pack it in and take Dodo back to safety. Well, I ask myself the same question. But when you've lived in a country, come to love the people, built up the place from nothing, you don't relish handing it over to a load of murdering Commies.'

'It can't be an easy decision.'

'No.' For the first time Teddy looked up, before his eyes were once more drawn back to the darkness as he scanned the circle of his estate. 'There's also the question of morale. Doesn't do for us Brits to be seen deserting our post. And yet . . .' He sighed, banging the palm of his hand on the balustrade and then wiping it down the side of his trousers. 'We'll have to get out in the end, of course. When independence comes, and we'll all be replaced by Malayans. But at least *that* is right and proper.'

'Yes.'

'So it'll be in order for me to leave your name with my solicitors?'

'Please do.'

'Can't thank you enough.' He tried to force a smile but failed. 'Dreadful imposition.'

'No, Teddy, it's not. I know it's stupid, but although

I'm no longer their leader, I still feel responsible for them.'

'I don't doubt,' he agreed, nodding his head up and down, before swinging round and staring into the room where everyone was having such a good time. 'Can't tell you what it means to Dodo, your all coming up to visit us like this. It can be damned lonely up here, don't think I don't know. Damned lonely.' And with a straightening of his shoulders he strode back into the party, picking up the words of the song as he slipped his arm round his wife's waist and smiled down at the top of her too brown hair.

Later, when they were lying in bed under their mosquito nets, Marion thought how like the camp it all was: the searchlights outside, the bars at the window, the night noises and dear old Bea in the next bed to hers.

'Bea?'

'Mmm?'

'Isn't it about time you thought of going home? I mean you won't be able to carry on at the Centre much longer now, will you? Only I've been thinking . . . I've got that great empty house in London, so why don't you move in with me?'

'Oh Marion . . .'

But Marion wouldn't allow Beatrice to finish, in case she said no. 'I know you'd hate to go back up North, and I could so easily convert the place, so you'd be quite separate and I promise you wouldn't lose your independence. And just think, it'd stop me hitting the gin whenever I get lonely! I really mean it, Bea.'

'I know you do, but you see I can't leave Singapore. At least not yet.'

'But Bea, Christina and Lau Peng can take over the Centre.'

'That's not the problem, it's Stephen . . . I doubt he'll last another year.'

'Oh, Bea! I didn't realise. I thought he was, well . . . just a bit senile.'

'No. Changi taking its toll.'

'But couldn't you bring him back with you?'

'He loves this country, so best to see his time out here. But thank you for asking. In other circumstances I might have jumped at it. Sleep tight.'

Under their separate mosquito nets, the two friends lay in the darkness thinking of what might have been.

In the next room the light was still on, and Kate lay on her bed watching Christina, who was sitting at the dressing table brushing her hair; and it crossed Kate's mind that this was the first time she'd seen it hanging loose since they'd said goodbye five years before.

'Christina, I know I asked you already, but why *don't* you wear your hair down?'

'I told you; it gets in the way.'

'Even so, I bet Lau Peng prefers it loose.' Then, the question Kate had been longing to ask slipped out despite herself. 'Will you and he get married?'

'At the moment we have other things to think about,' Christina told her, the strokes becoming faster as if she was angered by such a ridiculous question. 'So what about *your* love life, Kate.'

'Me? Oh I've been out with a few chaps, but nothing serious. It's finding someone with the same outlook, that's the problem – like you and Lau Peng. You don't know how lucky you are.'

'Yes I do.' For a moment Christina stared at her reflection, before once more brushing the beautiful hair that had to be disciplined just in case it might get in the way.

Dominica decided that for once she would leave off her night cream. After all, it had been such a very perfect day, that it seemed wrong not to look her best at the end of it.

She swung round on her stool, and smiled at the peaceful form of her husband, asleep in his favourite position: flat on his back, with one leg over the sheet as if at any moment he might leap up for work.

How very long it had been since they'd entertained,

and how splendid the dinner, right from the first course until the last, and how she had enjoyed planning it with dear Cookie. Really, the man was more of a friend than a servant, which was odd considering that she had never bothered to get to know any of her servants before. But then, she and everything else had been so very different with that pig of a first husband.

When she thought of what she had suffered, and how she had put up with it all those years, the way he'd gone drinking night after night, and then slinking off to the sordid brothels. No one would ever know the shame of her life then, when every slut that she passed might know what her husband demanded. No wonder she'd never envied them his so-called love-making, and the way he never washed when he fell into bed, and his breath stinking of drink and those filthy cigars. All she could be thankful for was that the Good Lord had spared her from bearing his child.

Very carefully she slipped under the sheet, examining dear Teddy's face and thinking how very lucky she was to have found him at last, and determined that now she had, she would never, never leave him. Not even if he begged her on his knees! *No*, her place was beside her husband; and if she was to die tomorrow, she would still have been blessed more than any other woman she had ever known.

Dominica leant forward and kissed Teddy's cheek, reaching under the sheet to find his hand as she snuggled down beside him.

Dear God, she prayed, and with a fervour that would have astonished her friends. When it is my time to be taken, please let me go before Teddy. I know I sound selfish – that I *am* selfish – but I just couldn't bear to be left without him.

Though she now spoke English, even in her thoughts, Dominica found herself murmuring a Dutch prayer that she'd learnt from her grandmother on the many visits she'd paid her; for, of the three daughters, Dominica was the one who could always be spared.

In the third room, Maggie was snoring gently, while Alice sat by the window, her nightdress pulled tight over her knees as she stared out into the night.

Beyond the bars, the searchlights blazed across the grass, draining the flowers of their colour as they stood like sentinels, their blooms still facing the West where the last rays of the sun had deserted them. And at the end of the tamed garden, an occasional glint betrayed the barbed wire that held back the jungle and all within it: mile upon mile, muttering, screeching, jabbering and whispering, but never for one moment betraying its secrets.

The next morning, Marion woke feeling ravenously hungry. This is ridiculous, she told herself, considering she'd stuffed herself silly the night before. Nevertheless, all she longed for was eggs, bacon, tomatoes, toast, marmalade and gallons of coffee, and possibly topped up with a mango or two! So instead of waiting for her cup of tea in bed, she dressed and went in search of Dominica.

She wasn't in the bungalow, and it was only when Marion glanced out of a window, that she spotted her sitting in the far corner of the verandah staring towards the road. It was so unlike Dominica to sit so very still, that Marion looked more closely, noticing her clasped hands, and her shoulders which seemed to be curiously ridged.

Sensing someone was behind her, Dominica turned, but after the usual morning greetings, she once more returned to her vigil, explaining that Teddy had just gone off on his rounds. 'And always it is the same: I sit here watching.'

Dominica was aware that she was not being a good hostess, so she forced herself to join Marion at the verandah, though when she tried to sound jolly somehow she couldn't; and she thought to herself that it was no good Marion staring at her like that, because she knew she was a sight and that a wife ought to look her best when waving goodbye to her husband, it was only that . . . 'Dominica! Teddy expects you to be a proper hostess, so be one!'

'At least today, Marion, I have all of you for company. And Sister Ulrica will be here soon.'

'Dominica, it must be a dreadful strain saying goodbye every morning.'

'Yes, Marion, it is. You see there are so many pre-cautions he has to take to avoid the bandits. Before, his habits used to be as regular as clockwork, but now he has to vary every single move or the Commies'll know where he is and murder him – just as they murdered poor Harry Smithson. And what is so terrible is that I never know where he is, so if he's injured, I won't know where to look and he could lie out there for hours – days even – bleeding and dying and crying out, and no one coming and . . .'

'He seems very capable, and his car *is* armoured, so I'm sure he'll come to no harm.'

'What do you damned well know,' Dominica retorted, suddenly feeling such a surge of anger that she could have spat.

How stupid of her to think that Marion and the others could understand, when they'd come from the safety of London, where the only danger was of being run over by one of those stupid British drivers? No, the only women who knew what they were talking about were in the front line like herself! Women like brave Lady Freda, who'd taught herself to shoot and make petrol bombs and had even designed a booby trap; but then, when it came to courage you could always count on the aristocracy or those who had once lived amongst them!

At which conclusion, Dominica swept past Marion without another word, entering the bungalow in order to supervise the breakfast for her bourgeois guests, and comforting herself with the thought that at least Dorothy had had the decency to stay on in Singapore.

7

Singapore

Dorothy woke up and stretched. And then she remembered: she was free! No resentful Maggie, no Marion, no Alice, no Kate, no Bea, and *no bloody Metro.*

She stepped under a cold shower, delighting in the sting of it and telling herself that the world was her oyster now that she had the suite to herself, and an attractive and like-minded friend to escort her wherever she wished to be taken. So what more could I want, she asked her reflection in the bathroom looking glass? To which the reply was – *everything!* Hell, she hadn't gone through the dreary respectability of growing up, and an oh-so-suitable marriage, plus years of imprisonment, not to gobble what was left: all that life had to offer: the best and even the worst.

Humming 'Don't Fence Me In', Dorothy sprayed herself with the scent she'd been given when she'd gone to Antwerp to buy a Japanese ceremonial sword; which, come to think of it, could even have belonged to Yamauchi! She smirked with satisfaction as she recalled his loss of face when he'd handed it over to the British officer. Not that the stupid man hadn't handed it right back again, but then officers always stuck together. Dorothy scrubbed her nails with a brush, brooding on the code that held fast most of the men who wore a uniform – possibly under the misapprehension they knew where they were, whereas civilians were such a very unpredictable lot. *She* especially!

Kicking aside the clothes she'd scattered the night before, Dorothy opened the wardrobe door. So what was to be her pleasure today? Was it to be the red two-piece she'd found at Wolland's, or the seemingly simple dress that had cost a fortune and was worth every penny. She pulled out the dress, selecting a pair of sandals, and deciding – despite the flattering way it nipped in her waist – that she was not going to wear her waspie; for if there was one thing she was sure of, it was that she would not be constricted in any way whatsoever.

After a leisurely breakfast on the verandah, and a call to her secretary to check that the business was running smoothly, Dorothy decided to have her hair done and then to visit Jake's flat in Farquar Street.

It was surprising that Dorothy noticed Jake at all, for she was paying off the driver of her taxi, and he and the policeman were hunched together in the shadow of a doorway on the far side of the street; and it was obvious by the way they stood with their backs to the passers-by, that neither of them wished to be observed.

Curiouser and curiouser, thought Dorothy, for the policeman was now hurrying away as if he wished to distance himself. What the hell was Jake up to, Dorothy wondered, ticking off the list of any of the many crooked deals that he might be up to: smuggling; shifting refugees to the mainland; currency or armament sales; flogging black market goods, etcetera, etcetera. The list was endless. And yet? He and the policeman had seemed in cahoots, and that certainly didn't add up.

Keeping out of sight by following in the wake of a family, who for some reason were all carrying bird cages, Dorothy drew level with Jake, who was now leaning nonchalantly against a shop window, and looking for all the world like an innocent abroad, which, thought Dorothy, he most certainly was not!

'So Jake? They finally caught up with you?'

With exactly the same aplomb as when she had caught him passing a note to the barman, Jake turned and doffed his hat.

'Morning, Miss Know-All.'

'And what have you been up to.'

'This and that.' And with a smile which failed to reach his eyes, he took Dorothy's hand and hurried her towards a rank of trishaws.

'I see you stuck by your decision not to go up to Dominica's.'

'As I said, Singapore also has its attractions.'

'Then why don't we look some of them up?'

'Right! So why not our godown where I first got into antiques?'

'And started to make your packet, don't you forget! So move your pins because you've got a very hard day ahead of you, Madam. And that's a promise!'

It was wonderful to bowl along the avenues and streets, the trishaw driver peddling through the cars and the carts and the people, as if his life depended on it; and when they arrived at the harbour, it was even better to be waved through the checkpoint by an official who saluted smartly.

It's all so easy with Jake, Dorothy thought, watching the muscles of his forearm as he pointed out the Customs House, and boasted that he knew every single official by name.

I bet he does, Dorothy told herself, *and* the names of every member of their families, *and* exactly how much they'd take to look the other way.

As they strolled round the harbour, Jake was greeted every few yards by the locals: pedlars, officials, soldiers, sailors, and the captains of the three yachts resplendent in their white uniforms, and who leant on the stanchions surveying the scene as if they alone were kings of all they surveyed.

'It might be good for business, but Christ I hate it.' Jake kicked an empty cigarette packet into the water, followed by the stub of his cigarette.

'What do you hate?' Dorothy asked, taken aback by a bitterness that surprised her.

'The changes. Before the war, this was a proud port serving the Empire, and what's more packed with *real* ships: liners, oil tankers, sail boats for local freight, plus the usual ubiquitous sampan. And now look at it! All right, so the bomb damage's been cleared and the wrecks blown up or towed out to sea, but . . .' He stared at the berths with contempt. 'Patched up out-of-date ships that nobody's proud of – least of all the crews; and the advance guard of the floating gin palaces and their tart-box motor boats; and, what's more, with not an honest-to-goodness sea captain amongst them.'

'What about those men in their splendid white uniforms?'

'Professional captains, hired by owners who don't know their aft from their stern. And for your information, the salute, my dear Dorothy, was because their bilges are stuffed with illicit goods that the said owners know not the what of, and that the likes of me knows *exactly* where to place.'

'Jake, why do you hate them so much?'

'Who knows? Except that once I was the only bad apple. Whereas now, now there is a positive bevy. Or, as an economist once put it with such depressing accuracy: bad currency always drives out the good.'

'Still don't see why you're that put out.'

'Schizophrenia, my poppet. The public school bit of me despising my fellows for letting in the riffraff; and of which I, Jake Haulter, was the Trojan Horse.'

The look that he threw her contained such bitter regret, that for the first time, Dorothy had an inkling of what Jake was really about: not the go-getter of the easy charm, but a far more complicated and dangerous animal; someone she knew she would never quite fathom even if she tried for the rest of her life. The knowledge so intoxicated her that she put it away for later, when she could give it her full attention.

'Jake, which of the warehouses is *our* godown?'

He pointed at random to the nearest, and Dorothy told him with some asperity that he was lying, and that he didn't know any more than she did; to which he agreed without apology, adding that it was possibly the one that had been burnt to the ground.

'Not since *we*'ve been here?'

'Certainly. Didn't make the press, of course. Or if it did, it was the usual play-down of three lines on the back page. I tell you, Dot, you don't know the half of what's going on.'

'Apparently not,' she told him, making a dig at his encounter earlier; but Jake didn't rise to it, for his attention had been caught by two men who had come into view: a surly and heavily built sea captain and a small Chinaman. They stopped in the lea of a crane, their heads so close together that they were almost ear to ear, and the Chinaman staring at his feet, which were encased in tan shoes laced with string.

'What's the matter?' Dorothy asked, for Jake continued to stare intently; but he didn't reply, grabbing her arm and pulling her into the shadows, while hissing at her to shut up because he needed to take a look; and when Dorothy made the reasonable suggestion that they moved a bit closer, he snapped back that he did *not* wish to be seen.

'Harry bloody Lime,' Dorothy flung at him, but again Jake failed to respond, for he was straining to hear what the men were saying – not that he could above the clatter of a ship being loaded, and a tanker weighing anchor.

When, a few minutes later, the men separated; the seaman hurried towards a Dutch freighter, while the Chinaman casually drifted behind a group of passing fishermen, just as Dorothy had done earlier.

'What the hell's going on,' Dorothy asked angrily, feeling as she did in the camps, when the heads of committees met together and she was barred. But Jake refused to tell her, only changing his mind when she had sworn blind that she wouldn't tell a soul, and had pointed out with some savagery that after all these years he must know her well enough to know she would never betray him. Even then he hesitated, staring down and examining her face, before at last telling her that he was almost sure that the Chinaman was a Communist agent. He then hurried on to explain that because of the Emergency and the increased incidents of terrorism in Singapore, the police had formed a new Special Branch which offered rewards to anyone with information leading to an arrest.

'Sounds exciting,' Dorothy whispered, glancing over her shoulder and feeling as if she was in the secret service herself.

'*Especially when you make a killing!*'

Something shivered inside Dorothy. It was as if she'd received an electric shock, and with a thrill that she wouldn't have thought possible, she recognised it for what it was: *Danger!*

And then she recognised something else. That this was what she had missed ever since her release from the camps: the risks of illicit deals when it would have meant the punishment hut or worse if she'd been caught; and through it all – even the sheer terror – that never-to-be-forgotten feeling of being alive!

With a shrug that threw off more than she knew, Dorothy acknowledged that everything she'd achieved since the war had been a substitute for what she was feeling now; for at last she acknowledged that danger was the drug on which she would always be hooked, and she embraced her dependence as if it had been a long-lost friend.

'So, Dorothy? And what would you like to do now?' asked the unknown quantity beside her.

She didn't look at him. She didn't need to.

'The same as you.'

'Ah.' Jake lifted his head and stared at an M.T.B. making for the open sea, his face as hard as the stone that they stood on. 'My place?'

'No.' Dorothy turned and led the way back. '*Mine.*'

The next second, Jake was grabbing her hand and

pulling her towards the street; his grip so fierce that Dorothy could feel his nails and the sharp edge of a ring.

'Raffles as fast as your legs'll carry us,' he shouted at the driver of a trishaw, and they tumbled in and were weaving in and out of the noonday traffic before they'd had time to right themselves. Neither of them looked at each other, but sat staring straight ahead as they willed the traffic police to wave them through; and when they turned into the Raffles driveway, Jake was paying the man before they had stopped.

Through reception they ran and the terrace restaurant and across the garden, taking the steps two at a time before thundering along the verandah, so that when they reached the suite, they were so out of breath that they were forced to sit on the step. And then everything became slow motion: Dorothy searching for the key before slipping it into the lock, and Jake stepping back politely as he pushed open the door.

'Jake, why don't you stay in here and pour us a drink?'

Dorothy disappeared through the curtain to the bedroom, and Jake turned and picked up a bottle of gin. But he didn't pour for some time. He just stood there staring down at the tray and wondering why there was a pulse in his throat, for it was something he hadn't felt since his first girl at the age of sixteen.

Betty, that'd been her name. Betty Pringle! All of eighteen, which made her an older woman! He remembered the frisson he had felt when he'd glimpsed her serving tea to his housemaster in her maid's uniform, and the first time he'd plucked up the courage to speak to her, which had been during half-term when the college was almost empty. Whatever he'd managed to stammer out, it must have done the trick, because they'd met in a scruffy café off the High Street – him an hour early of course and convinced that she would never come. But she had. And after a large tea, they had walked up the road towards Swindon, which just happened to be the direction of her father's cottage. They'd lain in a field until dusk, when she'd smuggled him up to her attic bedroom, and the paradise of her bed. God, but she'd been a frisky little number. He could still hear the sound of the squeaking bedsprings, which to his youthful ear had given the moment an added sophistication, albeit the added danger that her father would find them and he'd be put on report. Not that he hadn't been found out in the end, for he never could resist boasting; and the next day he had been expelled, his housemaster shoving him on the train back to his grandfather's with the ominous words: 'Unless you pull up your socks, Haulter, you'll most certainly come to a sticky end.'

And I probably will, thought Jake, selecting a glass. Unless, of course, the mythical rich widow picked him up and returned him to the style his public school had prepared him for, and for which he had never forgiven it.

'If you don't bring me that drink, I'll die of dehydration!'

Jake poured two gin and tonics, hooking his fingers over the glasses so that he could take the bottles with him, but when he elbowed back the curtain, he paused.

From the half-open shutters of the dressing room, the sun shot a hard bar of light across the tiled floor, the carpet, the jumble of débris, and finally across the bed on which Dorothy lay naked except for a string of pearls.

'Aren't you rather overdressed?'

Jake handed Dorothy her drink, placing his own and his wallet on the far bedside table before undressing, not quickly but with slow deliberation, lifting his head to undo his collar as the smoke from his cigarette rose upwards towards the fan.

'Budge up, Mrs Bennett. Or would you perhaps prefer the floor?'

They had luncheon in their room, and then dinner, sitting at a table under framed instructions of what should be done in case of fire.

'If I wasn't so tired, I'd suggest we returned to bed,'

Dorothy remarked, spitting out the stone of a peach, the juice dribbling down her chin and on to her stomach.

'Why don't we anyway – if only to test our self-control?

So they did.

'Dot? Glad you didn't go up-country?'

'I knew it'd be good.'

It had been more than that, it had been bloody perfect, the first time in her life that her head and body hadn't gone their separate ways. Always before, either her mind had raced ahead, or her body had wanted to be up and away, but this time . . .

'Dot? We should've done something about it five years ago. You know I fancied you even then.'

'Scruffy in the godown?'

He raised himself on his elbow, examining her matted hair and the fine down of her upper lip which was beaded with sweat. 'You look like the old Dorothy now.'

She rolled on to her stomach, half burying her face in a pillow covered in makeup. 'Jake, you're the only man who knows. You know – what I was.'

'Doesn't *he* know, your Alex-in-Fine-Arts?'

'Not even about the camps. Nor about Dennis. Nor Violet.' She made a sharp jerky movement, drawing her knees up to her stomach and hugging them. 'She'd have been nine years old by now.'

Jake held out his arm and Dorothy turned into it, pushing the hair back from her face and trying to smile but failing. 'That was another me,' she told him, 'the one who had children.'

'Child*ren*?'

'The other. The Jap guard and the abortion. *I told you.*'

'Yes. Yes, my darling, you did.' He held her even closer, feeling honoured that she had trusted *him*, when Alex-in-Fine-Arts still didn't know about anything. And he asked her what she got out of this relationship which sounded so very impersonal.

'It's a convenience. You can't have a full-time relationship *and* a career. Not if you're a woman. All right for a bloke,' she added bitterly. 'But if you're a girl you have to fit in, and find me the man who'd be that obliging.'

So he reminded her that he could be most accommodating as she should know by this time!

'You, Jake Haulter, live here in Singapore.'

'And at the moment so do you. So why don't we test our self-control a bit further? Give it a run for its money?'

And they did.

'I ask you, Dot! This is damned ridiculous, getting all dressed up at this hour of the night.' Jake was naked and hopping about on one foot trying to put on a sock which was inside out.

'Not if I feel like dancing, it isn't.'

'Give me strength!'

'Yes, please. Though I must say, you do look a bit washed out.'

'You cheeky bitch!' He made a grab for her and missed, chasing her round the table and through the dressing room and into the bathroom, where he cornered her in the shower.

'Now we're here we might as well wash,' he shouted, turning on the tap; and Dorothy laughed so much she slipped on the soap and refused to get up, so they sat facing each other, singing 'Hands, Knees and Boompsadaisy' with appropriate gestures, until the floor was flooded and they were forced to mop up the water with towels.

In the end they managed to look almost presentable, though anyone who looked too closely, would have known exactly what they'd been up to. Not that they gave a damn, for when it came to spitting in the eye of convention, *they* were both experts.

Unbelievably, once they were in the Tiffin room, they found that they were hungry again, so they ordered a lobster each, followed by chocolate mousse because everyone knows that sugar gives you energy, though in their case it was only enough for a single dance.

Later, when they sat under the stars drinking coffee,

it came to Jake that this was the very first time that he'd liked a woman as well as finding her attractive. 'Loved', yes, or even for his sins 'hated', but never before had he felt so completely at ease, and so much so that there was no need to put up a front.

'Dot, I think you'll have to come out on regular trips.'

Dorothy stretched her legs, hooking one foot over his. 'I've got a better idea. Why don't you come back and live in England?'

Jake lifted his feet on to the edge of an urn. 'Don't belong in England.'

'You were educated there.'

'Doesn't make me English. Just stops me from being anything else.'

'But it's changed. There's more room for . . . for . . .'

'Misfits like me.'

'Like *us*.'

'So what about your Alex?'

'He's got a wife. And besides, I'm tired of spending Christmas alone.'

'Mrs Bennett. Are you propositioning me?'

'*Yes*.'

'I see. Well, a man needs to be given time to answer. Needs to be – how shall we say? Courted!'

'So why don't we go where I can give it my full attention?'

The next morning they decided to have breakfast in the dining room in order to feel their way back into the workaday world; and the manager, who was squaring the balcony on the lookout for lazy staff, glanced down and thought what a handsome couple they made: the woman so sure of herself, and Jake – for whom he'd always had a sneaking regard – certainly had a great style. Unlike so many of his new guests from the old country, he told himself savagely, opening a cupboard in case someone was smoking within. They were nothing but jumped-up clerks and so-called executives who'd made their pile stepping into dead men's shoes.

As Dorothy opened her bag for a cigarette, she noticed the photographs she'd collected from the hotel's chemist.

'Here, Jake. Take a look. I think they've come out rather well,' she remarked. 'Especially this one of Alice, which Maggie must have snapped when she borrowed my camera.' She passed the photographs over, followed by another she hadn't noticed and which seemed to be of Lau Peng.

'Also in the market, I see,' Jake remarked, staring at the second photograph, and shading his eyes from the overhead light so that he could make out the details. 'Interesting. Lau Peng with his street library. Tell me, Dot, did he know it was being taken?'

Dorothy moved her chair closer, conscious of Jake's arm touching hers, and his warmth through the fine cotton sleeve. 'Doubt it. Or he'd be cheesing away like the rest.'

'Do you see who he's talking to?'

Dorothy peered at the picture, thinking that yes, she had seen the man before, but where? And then she remembered.

'It's the Chinaman! The one who was talking to the sea captain. The one you were so interested in watching.'

'Right! And Lau Peng is handing him – the *Commie* – a book.'

Dorothy refused to take in the implication . . . No, *not for one moment*. 'So what? Even Communists can read.'

Jake didn't reply, but she knew that look of old, right back to when he'd been working with the black marketeers and spotting an enemy had been a matter of life and death.

'Jake! You can't think that Lau Peng is in with them? Not the *terrorists*? I mean if there's anyone more anti-Communist . . . Besides, he works for our Bea!'

'And what better front? No, *listen*. What better than to get himself a girlfriend who's in with the people. Pretend to share *her* ideals, while all the time he's recruiting at evening classes, and then passing on information via an innocent street library?'

'*No Jake, it's not possible.*'

'Oh, come on! He wouldn't be the first person to do it. Why, only last June, two Chinese schools were closed because Security discovered they'd been running Communist cells.'

'But it's not a Chinese school, it's Joss's Centre.'

'Then poor old Bea.'

Dorothy grabbed the photograph and shoved it back into her bag, snapping the clasp shut before burying it in her lap.

'*I was thinking more of Christina.*'

8
Malaya

Sister Ulrica wondered why it was so very satisfactory to sing while driving a lorry. 'Five men went to mow, went to mow a meadow. Five men, four men, three men, two men, one man and his dog, went to mow a meadow!'

Perhaps it was a question of rhythm, fitting the music's beat to the turn of the engine? Whatever it was, this morning she was not only in good voice but good heart, for she was on her way to her friends, and her work at the resettlement village was progressing well.

Looking back over the past two years, it was hard to believe the shock that had greeted the Government's directive that all Chinese squatters were to be resettled in special protected villages. Why, ever since she or anyone else could remember, there had always been squatters; the poor souls driven to eke out a living on the edge of the jungle, where at least they could grow enough food for themselves and their chickens. Not that they had any right to the land, which of course belonged to the Sultans – at least in the eyes of the law – though God, she was sure, would view it in a very different light. And now, though it hardly seemed possible, their numbers had swelled to over half a million, because of the thousands of Chinese who had fled the towns during the Occupation, literally running for their lives because as everyone knew, the Japanese hated them more than any other race.

Poor Father Joseph, how he had exploded when he had first heard the Directive, pacing up and down the refectory and shouting at anyone who cared to listen, that the British were mad, and Sir Henry Gurney even more so. And yes, *of course* he knew that the squatters were supplying the bandits with food and information, but what else could they do when unspeakable acts had been committed in order to force them into submission. But to try and move the lot of them out of harm's way! It just couldn't be done!

But it *had* been done. And how very clever of Gurney to promise the squatters land that would be legally theirs. Not that there hadn't been problems, always would be with any directive that came down from above to those below, but on the whole it'd been a success, and *she* was helping to make it so. 'Six men went to mow, went to mow a meadow. Six men, five men . . .

Ulrica! How many times have you been instructed to guard against the sin of pride? It was not *she* who had made the success, but the Good Lord, of whom she was only a handmaiden and not a very good one at that! And how many times had her stubbornness and her love of getting her own way, stood in His path? If she was truly honest, ever since she could remember.

Ever since four, when Father Benedict had discovered her washing her doll in the holy water, and had dragged her by the ear to her mother, telling her that she was a wicked girl who would roast in the fires of Hell. Looking back, it was extraordinary how she had never doubted him throughout the whole of her childhood and her years as a novice. Indeed, it wasn't until Mother Teresa had arrived at the convent that the burden of terror had been lifted. 'My poor child,' she had exclaimed, striding down the path of the kitchen garden as if fast movement was an essential aid to profound thought. 'Fear is but the coward's vision of love, for you cannot love without faith, and faith is a leap into God's Kingdom, and must demand more of His servants than any terror you will ever be asked to face.' Of course, she had understood about the love, that she had found easy. But the faith! No, that had been the hardest task she had ever been set. For to trust was never to question, never to think except within the boundaries laid down by those set in authority over her.

Bitter had been her nights and her days of examination, and bitter her vision as she had searched for the comfort of a telltale sign in others. In fact, not until her internment had she begun to see that her submission to His Will was a glorious gift of freedom; a springboard from which she could release herself into the pure air of peace which was *beyond* understanding.

Truly, it had been a miracle, that first moment of revelation at the bed of a dying child; and it had touched everything and everyone around her, so that it had no longer mattered that Dorothy went with the guards, or that Beatrice was an atheist, or that Mrs Van Meyer was one of the most self-obsessed women it had ever been her misfortune to meet. No, then she had seen them for what they were: God's children, for whom the bitterness of experience had been too overpowering not to distort their vision. And from that moment on, she had loved them all, had found joy in the sharing of hardships because it had brought with it the gift of forgiveness.

'In the midst of death there is life,' Ulrica announced to the passing jungle, honking the horn as she took a sharp bend in the road. And sometimes more life and more love because of the very real danger that both might be lost.

Of course, her peace had not lasted, but then as Father Joseph had pointed out: goodness without temptation was like warmth without cold – you could not have the one without the other. Still, even when she had left her Order to go and work with the lepers, God had not turned away from her, only tempting her more, so as to make quite sure that she knew what she was doing and why!

Ulrica double declutched down to the third gear, taking another bend, and enjoying the pull of the wheel as the lorry tried to veer over, but was held firm on the brow of the road.

How beautiful was the jungle at dawn: the flash of bright birds soaring through the cracks of green foliage; and the points of sunshine zigzagging down between the leaves and the creeper, and across the back of the monkeys as they swung chattering between the branches.

Ulrica checked the compass attached to the dashboard. She must be careful now, for there were too many turnings that she could miss because of the undergrowth. With a practised hand she edged the gear lever back into fourth, listening to the slight knocking of the engine and wondering how long it would last before it gave trouble. Still, Sister Anna would know how to put it right, for hadn't she too discovered her vocation during internment, when the only book in her camp was on the workings of the internal combustion engine? Not that the priests had allowed her to tamper with *their* machines at the beginning, for after all they were only men, who would cleave unto themselves all that they believed to be theirs by right; just as the nuns had difficulty in trusting *them* to make up a patient's bed or even to brew a strong cup of tea!

May the good Lord be praised, not another check point! She must have come through a dozen or more, though this one would surely be the last before Dominica's.

Sister Ulrica slipped the gear into neutral and switched off the engine, coasting the last few yards to the patrol, in order to save Sister Anna's precious ration of petrol.

'Good morning, Sister.'

'Good morning. You wish to see my Identity Card?'

'Please.'

Sister Ulrica clambered down from the driving seat, thinking how creaky her bones had become, and how good it was of the Lord to send her to such a warm climate, instead of keeping her in Holland with all those horrible winters. She searched through her capacious pockets, producing an Indentity Card which she was ashamed to see had a fingerprint of butter in one corner. Still, all the policemen cared about was to be able to identify her from her photograph.

'Thank you, Sister. My men are just taking a look in the back of your lorry. Purely regulations of course, because I'm sure *you* wouldn't be hiding food for any bandits.'

'I have only this!' As if my magic, Ulrica produced a bottle of whisky, and the next moment was immediately filled with contrition, because she had paused for effect, instead of assuring the policeman that it was not for her but her friends.

'Ah. You are going to visit the British women at the Sungei Kuching Estate?'

'That's right. They are staying with my friend Mrs Forster-Brown. You see, we are all meeting for the first time in five years, so it will be quite a celebration!'

There was a loud bang on the lorry as a guard hit the side to show that the search was over.

'Everything is in order, Sister. I hope you enjoy your visit.'

'I'm sure I will. Goodbye, and may God be with you.'

Ulrica climbed back into the lorry, reminding herself that next time she went on a long journey, she must borrow a cushion from Father Joseph, who always kept a pile to serve as mattresses for the squatters' babies.

A few minutes later, Ulrica arrived at the plantation's turning, hooting to the guards who knew her well and waved her through. One more journey accomplished without any shootings, she told herself proudly; though as the lorry rattled along the drive, she was disturbed to see how many more rubber trees had been damaged deliberately. How very stupid it was for the bandits to destroy the wealth of their country, especially when Independence would come in the end, whether they held the British to ransom or not. But then, to be made to do anything by a foreign power – even to wait – must always lead to bitter unrest.

After all, even dear Joss – generally such a *sound* woman – had stubbornly refused to stop pinching wood from the Japanese huts, in the forlorn hope that they might collapse; when all that would have happened was that *they* would have been forced to do the repairs.

Dear, brave Joss, who was now with Our Blessed Lord in His Kingdom; how wonderful it was that the memorial that had been built with her money was such a splendid success in carrying on her work for the poor.

At last! If her memory served her right, round the very next bend would be the barbed wire fence and then the garden, and if she was very lucky a long cool drink; for it was all very well for Father Joseph to assure her that a habit was good protection against the sun, when all it did was to make her even hotter!

Beatrice had to admit that despite her forebodings, she was thoroughly enjoying herself; and not just because she was having a much needed rest from the Centre and Stephen, but because of the sheer luxury of Metro's bungalow. It had been a long time since she'd been brought breakfast in bed, and had had the time to wallow in a bath, let alone be waited on hand and foot. And now, here she was actually playing a piano that was more or less in tune!

Through the open window, Beatrice could hear the sounds of a lorry approaching, followed by Alice shouting to Metro that it must be Sister Ulrica arriving.

At last our party's complete, Beatrice thought with satisfaction, closing the lid of the keyboard because of the humidity, before feeling her way to the door, as she tried to remember where the chair was, and that damned jittery table. She had almost made it when she tripped, her spectacles flying off her nose and spinning Hell-for-leather across the floor as she fell with a thud.

'Knickers!'

This was all she needed, Ulrica to walk in and find her grovelling about at her feet like some sort of supplicant who had just seen the light!

As Ulrica clambered down from the driver's seat, it crossed Kate's mind how capable she looked, her strong brown hands gripping the door as she swung her feet to the ground with the practised movement of someone very used to a lorry, though only a few years back she hadn't even known how to drive.

'Hallo, my dears. *And Christina!* How wonderful that you were able to come after all.'

Marion picked up Ulrica's bag, which was full to bursting, a bundle of knitting catching the clasp, just as her crucifix used to catch in the sewing machine when they had worked in the factory making Japanese uniforms.

'Hope you had a good journey?'

'With God's help, yes indeed, Marion. You wouldn't think there was any Emergency the way I sailed through. In fact I was quite proud of myself. So? And where is our Dorothy?'

'For some reason Dorothy had to stay on in Singapore – business, I think she said, but she sent her love. Bea's here instead though, and Lau Peng's looking after everything at the Centre. In fact, we've had . . . *Oh my God!*'

The startled women followed Marion's horrified gaze to the back of the lorry, from which a stream of men were jumping! Young natives with hard angry faces, wearing filthy uniforms and carrying guns and pistols and machetes and sharp sinister knives; and running towards them and encircling them as they shouted to their leader, whose voice rose to a scream as one of the bandits broke away to round up the gardener. The terrified man stood transfixed, a fork still in his hand and his mouth wide as if it was trying to scream, while he stared towards yet another bandit who was tearing up the drive waving a knife covered in blood.

'*Dear God, where did they come from?*' Ulrica whispered, making the sign of the cross. But she knew already. As if from another angle, she could see the last checkpoint and the pantomime they had all been playing. The men hadn't been policemen at all, they'd been these terrible bandits, and when she'd shown her Identity Card and made her stupid remark, the men hadn't been searching the lorry but climbing into it! And if she could only have seen into the ditches on either side, *there* would have been the policeman, stripped naked and murdered, while *she* had driven the bandits past the guards and on to the estate.

'*What have I done?*' Ulrica heard herself shouting, Marion calling back to her to keep calm, whereupon the leader called her a British bitch, prodding her with a gun as he shouted '*No women speak.*'

Then, or so it seemed to Ulrica, everything splintered into separate tableaux: Metro calling to the houseboy to ring the alarm; a shot thundering past when the houseboy turned, his arm jerking upwards as he sank in a spiral to the ground; and all the time the bandits shouting and pushing them ever closer and closer, until it felt as if her breath was being hammered out of her body; and all the while her friends looking this way and that, as if they doubted their very senses.

'No,' Alice whispered, as she felt the foul breath of the Japanese on her, the guards shouting in the filthy language she couldn't understand so she wouldn't be able to obey; and then she'd be taken to Yamauchi and he'd lock her in the punishment hut, with the rats and the lice and the snails slithering over her and all around her, and her having to go to the lavatory, and all the stinking smells . . .

'*Mummy! Mummy! Where are you?*'

'This is absurd,' Beatrice told herself, aware of how ludicrous she looked crouched down like some baby learning to crawl. The specs couldn't have disappeared off the face of the earth, for goodness' sake, so they must be in the room somewhere. All she had to do, if only she kept her head, was to be calm and to *think*. Now. The light coming from the left must be from the window, so Q.E.D. all you have to do is to crawl back on your tracks and start again. Just so long as Ulrica didn't . . . *Surely that was a shot?*

Beatrice! Pull yourself together. It's only one of Teddy's guards practising with his rifle, so just you concentrate on what you're doing, instead of . . .

'Women stand line! Stand. Or be shot!'

It was a Tenko!

This time Beatrice understood exactly what was happening: they'd been raided by the terrorists! They'd got her friends and were shouting at them to stand in line, pointing their guns at their stomachs, perhaps even . . . *No.* Don't let yourself think about that, think of . . . *They'd be coming up here to search the bungalow* and if she didn't hide bloody quick she'd be murdered like all the rest of them.

Turning yet again, Beatrice scrambled back the way she had come, catching her knee in her skirt and falling between the legs of the piano as she dragged herself under.

If only she could control her breathing; not that it wasn't to be expected, being purely a reaction to shock, and nothing to do with the panic that they were out there somewhere, and soon would be coming to find her. Now. Take a deep breath and try to calm yourself, you stupid woman. After all, you've been in many worse plights than this. *But not without your specs.* Not without being able to see where the bastards were.

Dear God. Someone . . . was . . . coming . . . up . . . the . . . steps. Coming through the hall. *Coming into the room.* Closer and closer and closer. *Stopping!* But *why* had they stopped? They had stopped because they were listening!

Beatrice pushed her knuckles into her mouth to stifle the sound of her heart beats, for they were all she could hear, on and on and on, boom, boom, boom.

Now *listen.* All that's happening is that you're playing a game of hide-and-seek and that's only your sister standing out there. It's only stupid old Olive trying to trick you into giving yourself away, and you know she's no good at the game even with father helping, because you've always managed to . . .

I can see his legs! He's lifting something off the top of the piano. He's turning round. It's . . . it's not possible. He's walking out! The bandit is walking out of the room because *he hasn't spotted you.*

But why are there more men in the hall? And what are they calling out? And why that scream? And what's that scuffling noise and that thud, and why are they shouting so loud?

And why did I never learn Chinese?

Then, as suddenly as the feet ran up the steps, they were running down them again; the sharp sound of the boots heavy on the concrete, but nevertheless growing quieter all the time, until at last a blessed silence descended.

No. Wait a second, Beatrice. Couldn't one of them have been left behind? Left to guard perhaps, and standing very still and waiting and watching, just in case?

Again Beatrice caught her breath, but the silence held, and she knew with that sixth sense given to those who cannot see, that she was alone. She was blind and alone in the empty bungalow, while out there somewhere were all her friends, who were most likely dead or even now dying in pain.

Beatrice rubbed the palms of her hands down her skirt, trying to wipe off the sweat which seemed to be trickling from every pore of her body, so that she had to lift up her skirt to unstick it from off her thighs.

All right, so she was more or less blind, but she still had the rest of her senses, so there must be something she could do before they killed her as well. *The guns in the rack in the hall.* No, don't be a fool, the men would have grabbed them, it would have been one of the first things they'd have done, but *what about the telephone*? It would be easy to miss the telephone in the excitement of finding those firearms, and she knew exactly where it was because of her call to the Centre. It was on the small table, so all she had to do was to follow her nose. It was perfectly simple.

Suddenly sure of herself, again Beatrice crawled across the floor; and this time she managed to find the door, where she paused, sitting back on her heels and listening intently.

Nothing.

Nothing, except for the hum of the electric plant and the shriek of those terrible voices, except . . . It wasn't possible! *Some of the voices were women.* They were alive! Only please, *please* don't let them be wounded or raped or any of the things she'd read in the papers, let alone all the stories that had been whispered . . .

Why the Hell are you sitting here, when you should be calling for help?

With infinite care and keeping down low because of the view from the verandah, Beatrice edged her way across the hall, always alert for the sound of returning footsteps, and telling herself that if they did come back she'd crouch behind the door, and if she . . .

Someone had dropped a shoe.

Beatrice's hand travelled up from a foot to a leg to a skirt, and then over a soft sticky mound to the side of a twisted neck, her fingers pushing aside a thin chain and resting on an artery, while her head bent to one side as if she was listening. There was no pulse. And because of the chain, she knew that it was Metro's ayah who had screamed as the terrorists had killed her.

'I *must* get to the telephone,' Beatrice heard herself muttering, crawling round the body and an arm flung across her path, until at long last her groping hand found the leg of the table and travelled upwards.

The ornament only rocked. Then it tipped sideways and toppled on to the floor, its thunderous crash echoing through the passages and the nine deserted rooms: through the bedrooms cluttered with clothes and half-finished letters; through the dining room with its bowl of orchids and its open box of cigarettes; through the drawing room, with its table laid for a meal; and through the kitchen, now scattered with vegetables and the shell of a broken egg; and as the sound swept on its remorseless course through the doorway and out into the passage, it passed over the body of Cookie, his hands still clutching a spoon and a slice of lemon.

It was very hot in the garden, the sun sucking up the moisture so that the earth had faded from brown to a thin grey. It had even drained the watering can that stood to the side of a bed of roses, the heads hanging as if in mourning for the gift that had been snatched from their roots.

The women too were wilting, some of them swaying as they stood in line staring towards Christina, who had been pulled out from their ranks to translate for the bandits and their leader. Now she was listening intently to their instructions, before telling her friends what was demanded.

Dominica shifted her gaze from Christina to the drive, dreading and yet hoping for the return of her dear Teddy's car. And as she watched, she was amazed by how calm she felt, even while she told herself that whatever terrible things the bandits did to her, she must never tell them where her husband had hidden the ammunition.

If only she could hear the car before the bandits, she might even be able to create a diversion, and then at least Teddy would have some chance of getting away. Not that he would. He'd come driving even faster towards them, and the bandits would shoot him dead, just as she'd always imagined for all these terrible years.

Dominica was diverted as a murmur ran through the line, and she turned to watch Christina nodding to the leader before stepping forward to tell them what the bandits had instructed.

'He wants to know which of us the house belongs to?'

'*I* am Mrs Forster-Brown,' Dominica announced to the leader, before turning and raising her voice to Christina.

'Kindly inform the men that if they dare lay a finger on any of us . . .'

'Dominica, *please*,' Christina begged. 'Don't you understand, he wants to know where your husband keeps the ammunition?'

May the Good Lord give me His strength, Dominica prayed, knowing that moment she had been dreading had finally arrived. The moment when she would discover if she was a fit wife for her dear brave Teddy.

'Tell the bandits there is no ammunition in the house.'

'But it's no use, Dominica. *He knows*. One of the servants must have told him.'

'Then you must tell him the servant is lying.'

Even as Christina translated, one of the men stepped forward and struck Dominica such a blow that she almost fell.

'Please, Dominica, you *must* tell him,' Christina pleaded. 'We'll all be all right if we only do what we're told.'

But Dominica remained silent, discovering a glory that she had only glimpsed on the many occasions since the war when she had stretched the truth, had embroidered it here and there, or had even transferred it whole in order to tie *her* body to the stake, so that the audience would at last understand what an amazing heroine lived within their midst.

So Dominica continued to stand without moving or saying a word. Just as years of reprisals kept the rest of the women in line, only their eyes betraying what they felt when a bandit grabbed hold of Alice and dragged her in front of them, screaming. And when she continued to scream, the sound mingled with all the other screams that the women had been forced to hear, and they still remained silent and riveted to the ground, and who's to say whether it was because of their training or because of the fear for their own lives?

Even Sister Ulrica couldn't move, though she prayed to God to give her the strength to deliver the girl from the hands of the enemy. Then, suddenly, as one of the bandits raised his machete high over Alice's head, strength was given to Ulrica to run forward, her arms outstretched and the back of her headdress streaming behind her like the veil of a bride.

'No. Stop! Let it be me.'

The shot rang out across the garden and into the jungle, lifting the screeching birds high into the air, where they hovered for a second, before turning and streaking towards the horizon.

Ulrica lay, her arms still outstretched towards Alice, as the leader screamed at Christina to tell her friends that if any other woman dared move, they would be shot like the stupid nun. So the women fell back into line, staring into the barrels of the guns as the leader again demanded to know where the ammunition had been hidden.

'Under our bed. Under the floorboards.'

The tears streaked down Dominica's face, mingling with the mascara that she had put on with such care only a few hours earlier.

Then, once Christina had translated Dominica's words, all was movement as the bandits divided into two groups: the smaller group taking Dominica and their translator up to the bungalow; while the rest of the men remained where they were in order to watch the women; the women who stared at the red star spreading ever wider across Ulrica's shoulder; just as the red star of the terrorists had spread throughout the villages and hamlets that they had taken by force – at whatever the cost to themselves or those who stood in their path.

Since the sound of the second shot, Beatrice had grown almost hysterical; repeatedly jiggling the telephone rest as she tried to get through to the exchange. She even shook the receiver, banging the telephone with her fist, but the line remained stubbornly silent.

'Where guns he is? You tell.'

What *are* they shouting about, wondered a desperate Beatrice, because she had crawled over and checked that they had taken the guns from the hall. Then she remembered Dominica mentioning in Raffles that Teddy had hidden a secret store somewhere in the bungalow.

Oh my God, they *couldn't* be coming back? *Surely not again?* Not more hiding and cat and mouse, and watching that shadowy outline of legs?

Beatrice was still kneeling on the floor clutching the receiver and jiggling the rest, when what seemed like an army of dim figures, darkened the doorway.

It was the bandit leading the group who first caught sight of Beatrice – now flattened against the wall – and the words he'd been shouting stopped in mid-sentence as he raised his pistol and took aim.

It was Christina, shouting in Chinese and in such a severe and commanding tone, that made him lower the barrel. That, and her running to the severed flex and holding it up, which must have saved Beatrice's life; though everything happened so quickly and in such a mist, that it was only later that she understood that, but for Christina, she would have been shot and lying dead.

Incredibly, during the entire action, Dominica remained staring down at her ayah and friend, as she wondered why she looked *so* small and defenceless, when she had always filled every room she entered, with her sense of fun. Why wasn't she jumping up and telling them that it was all a big silly joke, instead of lying there in that funny position because she was dead?

'Dominica, we *must* show the bandits where the ammunition is hidden.'

Dominica nodded towards Christina, before turning and leading the way into her bedroom, where she pointed to the no-longer-secret hiding place of her husband. It will all be the same in a hundred years, Dominica told herself, staring at Teddy's photograph, and remembering all the many things she had never said.

It was a long time before Christina and Dominica emerged from the bungalow; the bandits behind them, laden not only with ammunition but with food, and shouting and beaming as they held up the spoils to their comrades, who were still guarding the white bitches who stood in line.

'You are lucky not to be shot,' the leader shouted at the women, but they didn't look up for they were staring at their dear friend spreadeagled and bleeding on the ground.

Then, as suddenly as the terrorists had arrived, they left. With a final glance around the garden and up to the bungalow, they turned and made for the jungle; one of them dragging a leg of meat, which could just as easily have been the head of a man, as had happened only a few days earlier.

The moment the bandits were out of sight, Alice's sobs became hysterical.

She sobbed as the women rushed to Ulrica, and she sobbed when they said she was alive. Indeed, it was the sound of her sobbing which forced Beatrice on to the verandah; for she had sat without moving ever since Christina had saved her life.

In the end, she couldn't bear the sound of Alice's cries a moment longer, and despite the likelihood of being shot, she felt her way out of the hall and down the first few steps to the garden. That was the eeriest moment of all: her friends rushing past and shouting that Ulrica was wounded but alive, and yes, they were all alive, and yes, the bandits had gone; and then disappearing up or down, and leaving her clinging on to the balustrade, unable to stop anyone for long enough to make any sense out of anything.

If I believed in Hell, this would be it, thought Beatrice; the shadowy figures coming and going as if in a nightmare, their voices seeming as distorted as they did, as they shouted for bandages, blankets, iodine, water and lint.

Finally, Beatrice sat down to wait, while she brooded on how it would be for the rest of her life. This is what blindness is all about, she told herself. It's having to wait for other people; having to be patient while the rest of the world gets on with its life.

It seemed to Beatrice to be hours later that Alice placed her spectacles in her hand, and with some ceremony she put them on, savouring the moment when *something* would come into focus. Yes, there was Alice, shaking from head to foot if she wasn't mistaken, and her poor little face swollen from crying.

'So *there* you are, Alice.'

'Yes.'

'And how are you feeling?'

'A complete idiot.'

'Huh! You're not the only one, so be a good girl and tell me what's going on?'

'Well.' Alice drew in a still shaky breath and spoke very fast. 'The servants are all wounded or dead, and Ulrica was shot but *she's* not dead. And Kate's doing her best with bandages and stuff. And Marion's going to drive her to hospital, and Metro's going with her to show her the way. And I don't know what the others are doing, and if only I could do something, I wouldn't feel so bad, but I don't know what.'

'I can tell you what,' Beatrice informed her briskly. 'You can help me down these steps, and while we go you can fill me in on all the details, because nothing's worse than not knowing what the Hell's going on. And you can take my word for that!'

So Alice told her, and when they got to the lorry, an unconscious Ulrica had already been lifted into the back, Kate cradling her in her arms, as she wiped her forehead and neck.

'Marion?' Beatrice shouted up to her friend, who was stacking extra bandages in case Ulrica had another haemorrhage.

'May I come too? I know there's nothing I can do, but I would like to be with her.'

'Of course.'

Marion helped Beatrice into the lorry, before jumping

down and checking the tyres, and then climbing into the driving seat beside Dominica, who sat like a statue staring towards the drive.

Whether it was the movement of the lorry, or Beatrice taking Ulrica's hand, no one could decide, but suddenly Ulrica's eyes fluttered and then opened wide.

'Beatrice!' she whispered. 'Then I am not in Heaven.'

Despite everything that had happened, Beatrice began to laugh, and then Kate was laughing and shouting the remark through the slit window to Marion and Dominica; and even Ulrica managed a half-smile before once again slipping into unconsciousness, Beatrice still holding the strong brown hand which now seemed to be so frail.

Through the whole of that long journey, Beatrice crouched by Ulrica holding her hand, while she stared down at the familiar face which now looked all of its sixty-five years. We're growing old, she admitted to herself; and she glanced at Kate, remembering how young she'd been when she had first reported to her ward, in those halcyon days before the war.

We've survived over nine whole years together, she told herself triumphantly, and life's not over yet. No, not by a long chalk! And eyes or not, she was damned glad that Christina had stopped that bandit from finishing her off – if only that she'd be able to see Kate following in her footsteps; which, though they might falter, would do their darndest to keep on keeping on.

Three miles out from the garden, Dominica spotted Teddy returning, and she literally screamed at Marion to stop the lorry, jumping out before it *had* stopped, and flinging herself in front of Teddy's car and finally into his arms.

When he'd been told what had happened, first by Dominica and then by a calmer Marion, they continued on their separate ways: the lorry to the hospital, and Teddy to the workers' living quarters to check that they were safe.

They had been driving for some time before Dominica

muttered that whatever Marion might have assured her earlier, if she hadn't been so stubborn about the hiding place, Ulrica might never have been shot! So Marion reassured her again, ending by complimenting Dominica on her courageous stand, however terrible the outcome. There was a brief silence while Dominica wiped her tears, before she accepted that *perhaps* she had acted for the best, for everyone knew that terrorists were just like the Japs, and therefore *quite* unpredictable. In fact, now she came to think about it, if she had told the bandits the moment they had asked, they could have shot everyone in their excitement. So really the stand she had taken had most likely saved everyone's life! Indeed, on deeper reflection, she was quite sure that she'd done the right thing, if only as an example to Alice, who was still at that impressionable age when an older woman's courage could affect the whole of the rest of her life!

Having satisfied both her conscience and her ego, Dominica spent the rest of the journey chattering on about all the other heroic moments that they had lived through; about the dreadful Van Meyers, and wasn't it lucky that she no longer bore their name, for she wouldn't wish to add to *their* glory; and that the moment they arrived at the hospital she must drive the lorry stright back to the bungalow, so as to assure her dear Teddy that she had done the right thing.

Then, for some reason only known to herself, Dominica lectured Marion on the lives of the blessed Saints, and how of course *her* Christian name was of great religious significance; until Marion wondered at the blindness of love, and in particular the blindness of the husband of this saintly woman who was now munching her way through a whole bar of chocolate.

The hospital corridor possessed a merciless efficiency that brooked none of the muddle of the people it was designed to serve.

The lights beneath their white enamel shades marched in a relentless line from the entrance to the doors of the operating theatre, their brilliance emphasising the white walls which, at a height of exactly five feet, gave way to even shinier tiles, that were broken at measured intervals by the frosted glass of the doors that distorted rather than explained the shadowy outlines within.

A strong smell of disinfectant pervaded the whole: Jeyes fluid rising from the polished linoleum floor; and a subtler and more sinister smell which seeped from the hidden wards, and which spoke of wounds and the cloudy liquid that lay in wait to sting even while it destroyed.

With one exception, the mahogany benches were empty, as if an unknown hand had tidied away the occupants; and in some mysterious fashion, the three women who occupied the bench nearest the operating theatre only managed to emphasise rather than break the symmetry of the whole.

A nurse who was loading a trolley with linen thought how patiently the women waited, neither fidgeting nor leaving their seat, and it crossed her mind that they sat with exactly the same resignation as natives. But then, Marion, Beatrice and Kate had learnt to wait in the hard school of a conquered race, albeit for less than four years; however, a docile acceptance is bred not from any length of time but from a dogged sense of how to survive.

They've got to be British, the nurse assured herself, though there was a passiveness about the women that she found vaguely unsettling, so that when she finished loading the linen, she pushed the trolley too close to where they were sitting, forcing them to pull up their feet in order to avoid the wheels.

'How much longer?' Kate asked for the third time, thinking of the nights she'd spent in the sick bay hoping against hope for a patient's recovery.

'It's a chance to rest,' Beatrice reminded herself, watching the nurse trying to negotiate a door, and wondering why she hadn't ticked her off for her lethal way with the furniture. 'I tell you, what with the Centre and Stephen, I'm lucky if I even get a snack on the trot.'

It was Marion who alerted the others to a sister emerging from the operating theatre; and they stood and waited in silence as she swept towards them with that superior expression only given to those who know something that others don't.

'I'm glad to tell you that your friend has come through the operation,' she began, sweeping them with a smile which appeared to possess at least three rows of teeth. 'We removed the bullet, and given her age, there is no reason why she should *not* recover, though it'll take some time and we *must* guard against any untoward complication.'

As Beatrice made a move towards the recovery room, the sister lifted her arm and barred the way. 'I'm sorry, but our patients *never* receive visitors on the day of an operation. Tomorrow perhaps. Though we'll have to see, and so long as it's one only. And please remember that the visiting hours are between six-thirty and seven in the evening, and at no *other time whatsoever*, is that clearly understood?'

The explosion began with a deceptive quietness, as if a volcano was having some trouble erupting; but, like a volcano, it grew in strength until the tiles echoed in the wake of its fury.

'Now you listen to me, Sister What-ever-your-name is. I am a doctor of some twenty-three years' standing; a doctor who has, in the course of her professional life, officiated at more operations and in more diverse circumstances than *your* lack of imagination could ever envisage in a month of Sundays. And because of these qualifications, not to mention a personal obsession with the so-called compassion of our calling, I wish to point out that you do not come it high and mighty with *any* relative or friend who is sick with worry about any other relative or friend who might have the misfortune to land on one of your sterilised tables. And that whatever the visiting hours, I and my colleagues will make quite sure that our dear and treasured Sister Ulrica will have as much of our company as *she* thinks fit; if only in order to give her the strength to withstand a regime that bears all the hallmarks of a rampant dictatorship. *Do I make myself clear?'*

With a glare that had once quelled a whole phalanx of sisters, Beatrice turned on her heels and steamed towards the administration office, so that it was all that Kate and Marion could do to keep up with her and avert her crashing into a door or a misplaced wall. Indeed, it was only when she had made her wishes clear to not one but three of the hospital hierarchy, that Beatrice allowed herself to be led from the building and to be given a restorative drink in a nearby hotel. Even then, she continued to rumble ominously, reminding her friends and anyone else within hearing, of that absolutely ghastly Doctor Trier in Camp Two; and did they remember *her* bloody high-handed way of dictating, not to mention her vindictive visiting hours; which, incidentally, had been started by that bitch of a Florence Nightingale, who'd spent her life putting staff above patients, and who's only real concerns were her time-tables and the complications of her blasted plumbing!

In the end, Beatrice could not but help notice Marion and Kate trying desperately not to smile, and despite her incensed condition, she too began to laugh until she was roaring and slapping the table, while her friends weren't at all sure if she wasn't just plain drunk or hysterical with relief.

The journey back to the plantation was a never-to-be-forgotten ride, the three of them squashed together in the front of the lorry singing their heads off: 'The Sun Has Got His Hat On', 'All Things Bright And Beautiful' and many others, including a very lewd version of 'Waltzing Matilda' – and this from Kate who was usually so prissy. Finally, they were forced to stop, not only because Marion had lost her voice, but because Beatrice – who was wedged in the middle – announced that her so-called friends had irretrievably damaged her ear-drums.

"Course you know *why* we're behaving like this,' Kate remarked, lifting her feet and resting them on the dashboard. 'It's the relief after all that's happened. In fact I'm sure I've read somewhere, that when anyone's been close to death, they always react by either making a joke or making love.'

At the mention of love, each of the women thought of Dominica; who, had they but known it, was brooding on the very same subject.

Dominica and Teddy stood on the verandah, staring into the night. They wore their dressing gowns and slippers; a solid middle-aged couple who looked more suited to the calmness of the suburbs rather than the rigours of a country at war.

'I was *so* frightened all the time those bandits were here,' Dominica whispered, her husband slipping her arm through his, and muttering 'My poor darling' as he patted her hand.

'But all the time I kept on asking myself what my dear husband would do,' she continued, adding almost shyly how very much she loved him.

Teddy turned and smiled at his wife, a very ordinary and exhausted man, though at that moment he looked neither. He looked what he really was: a man blessed with the gift of acceptance, for he loved as he found; and in that loving achieved a greater happiness than any of his more intelligent and sophisticated compatriots who, because they were always searching for faults, invariably found them.

'Isn't it time we went off to bed,' he suggested, and his wife nodded her approval; while at the same time wondering at her ability to put the deaths of Cookie and her ayah behind her; and at that moment, not very much caring why.

'Tomorrow we shall spoil ourselves!' Dominica stated firmly, leading the way into the bungalow, and closely followed by Mr E. V. Forster-Brown, Manager of the Sungei Kuching Estate, and husband of the perfect Dodo, who had done him the supreme honour of becoming his wife.

9
Singapore

During the days and nights that Jake and Dorothy spent together, they made love nine times, went out for four meals, had three blistering rows; and all in all not only thoroughly enjoyed themselves, but found a companionship that neither of them would have believed possible.

All right, so they were very alike, but that didn't entirely explain what had happened. It was more to do with trusting each other, which in Jake's case hadn't happened since the age of six when he'd discovered that nanny had lied about Father Christmas; and in Dorothy's case had been the moment when the Japanese had marched her husband over the hill and shot him. But now, suddenly and unexpectedly, they were like two children who had discovered the sandy beach where the tide did *not* come in to wash away the sandcastles; and, like all sand that is left long enough, they were dimly aware that something was setting solid.

Not that they acknowledged the fact, for they chose to keep a certain distance; and if they did have the odd flights of fancy, then they would firmly drag each other back to earth, if only to savour the moment when one or other of them thought it might be more amusing to leave it.

'You won't be able to stay here tonight,' Dorothy remarked from her bed, enjoying the precise movements with which Jake did everything, even to knotting his tie. And then, almost as an after-thought, she added that

Maggie would be back and she didn't fancy a threesome, deliberately trailing her coat because touching boundaries was what they enjoyed almost better than anything else.

Jake peered at himself in the glass, catching Dorothy's reflection and winking, which could have meant anything and probably did.

Shrugging on his jacket, he crossed to the bedside table and picked up his wallet, remarking that there was always his place, as he automatically checked the contents. 'Incidentally, someone will have to tell Bea about Lau Peng and the Communist, not to mention what he's most likely been up to!'

Amused at his giveaway gesture, which Dorothy took as a signpost to his past rather than a personal insult, she wandered into the bathroom, picking up her lipstick and writing £1,000,000 across her stomach, before spraying the last of her scent on her hair.

After a heated discussion on the merits of a shower versus a bath, they had breakfast on the verandah, Dorothy writing a letter and Jake hiding behind *The Times*. Just lately he'd got into the habit of checking the obituaries for his grandfather's name, though he was never quite sure whether he wanted to see it, or whether he dreaded the moment when it would be too late for the old man's forgiveness.

'John Simon Barnstaple, beloved father of Elizabeth and George . . .'

He wondered at the surname. Had the family originally come from Devon, or was the 'Barn' part of it more telling? Tipping the paper, he stared at the top of Dorothy's head which was now bleached blonde because of the sun. 'Dot? Why do you never mention your father? What was he like?'

'Like?' Dorothy thrust the letter away from her and reached for a cigarette.

'Tallish. Brown eyes. Scrupulously clean. And occasionally given to bashing.'

'How d'you mean?'

'Like me.'

'*You?*'

'As long as I can remember.'

'So you didn't love him?'

'Oh yes. I loved him all right, which was *his* reason for the clouts.'

She blew out the smoke, nudging the ash off the cigarette with the tip of her finger. 'You see he couldn't forgive me. Not when he knew he was worthless.' And suddenly she saw that another piece of her jigsaw had fallen in place. 'So let's get down to reception and post my letter. Or it'll be arriving home before I do.'

As usual, reception was milling with people booking in or passing through: soldiers in mufti, planters and their wives taking a break from The Troubles, and the new breed of commercial travellers that had now begun to appear: thin precise men with thin precise cases and mouths to match.

Alice was the first to spot Dorothy through the crowd, Maggie and Marion trailing behind her with their luggage. 'Look, there's Dorothy!' she shouted, rushing forward as if they'd been separated for years.

'Hallo, you lot. Had a good time?'

There was a heavy silence, followed by Maggie spitting at her that it had been *ruddy marvellous*; and then bursting into a fit of laughter that sounded as hollow as her mother's, when anyone had asked her if her consumption was on the mend?

It wasn't until the friends were settled in Dorothy's suite, that she managed to get a coherent story out of them; and when they started to tell her about the raid and what had happened, an odd irritation grew inside Dorothy, for she felt that they had no right to experience anything violent when she wasn't there. However, the feeling dissolved into one of sheer panic, when she heard that Ulrica had been shot. She could hardly bear to listen to the details, and yet she made Marion repeat them over and over again.

Her own Sister Ulrica injured and in danger! The best friend she had ever had, in that bloody hospital with God-knows-who poking around inside her. And when Maggie told her not to worry, because Ulrica was being transferred to the Alexander Hospital where they could keep an eye on her, all she could think of was that it was the same hospital in which Joss had so suddenly died.

Not that she mentioned her fear, because her feelings for Ulrica were too precious to be exposed to anyone. Instead, she excused herself and ran into the bathroom, sitting on the lavatory and crying, and then stopping and then crying again; which was ridiculous, she told herself, considering how very tough she had always been. So she brooded on how the raid had been managed, and the more she thought about it, the more it didn't add up. So she returned to her friends, and asked them how the bandits had been able to slip into the lorry in the first place?

'Under the pretext of searching,' Marion explained, thinking how white Dorothy looked, and with that odd downward set to her mouth which always boded trouble for someone.

'All right. But how did they *know* Ulrica was coming? At *that* time, and on *that* day?'

Alice, who had been wondering the same thing, turned to Marion who always seemed to know the answer to everything. 'And how did they know she was on the way to *that* plantation?'

'Which just happened to have a secret store of ammunition!' Maggie added, for the first time voicing a suspicion that had been niggling her ever since.

'One of the servants must've been involved,' Marion told them firmly, reassuring herself as much as anyone else, because Teddy had told her that he didn't think any of the servants knew. 'After all, no one else was aware of the secret store except us.'

'Someone else did know,' Dorothy shouted, angered by an innocence that made them so stupid. '*Someone* knew the arms and ammunition were there, and *that*'s why they raided. And what's more . . .' She drew in a deep breath, taking her time to break the news, because she wanted to savour the moment before they too would be disillusioned. 'I might just know who it was!'

By the time Kate and Beatrice arrived at the Centre, they were exhausted, especially Beatrice, whose outburst at the hospital had drained her more than she would have thought possible; and that, despite a good sleep and breakfast carried back to bed.

Not that she wasn't used to being exhausted, especially the last few months; though the sudden flash of her old spirit had left her not only drained, but with a depression which was the worst she had ever known. It was all very well slogging her guts out at the Centre, but it was no stoker of fires that was for sure; and it crossed her mind that her battle with the Sewage Department contained elements of therapy in it, as well as contributing to the wellbeing of Singapore.

As so often in the past few years, Stephen's reaction to their early return and the story of the raid had been unpredictable. After an initial resentment that they had returned early and that his peace had been shattered, he became almost his old self, much enjoying the reversal of roles as he cooked a meal, while Beatrice and Kate sat on the balcony recovering.

'Quite like the old days,' he told himself, bursting into a few bars of 'The Road to Mandalay', as he wondered if he'd put any salt in the omelette, and then telling himself that they were too tired to care.

'I suppose you know I was on cookhouse duty in Changi,' he shouted to the women on the balcony. 'In fact the things I could do with grasshoppers'd make your minds boggle. Not to mention your stomachs!'

Carefully he divided the omelette into two equal slices, slipping the portions on to the plates and waiting for the women's congratulations. But they were too preoccupied to do anything except move to the table and eat, though Stephen was pleased to note that he had been right about the salt.

Afterwards, Kate and Beatrice returned to sit on the balcony, each of them deep in their own thoughts.

How strange it is, thought Kate, that despite all that's happened, I keep on thinking of Duncan. After all, we hardly know each other, and yet . . . Where was he now, and what was he up to? Was he in Out Patients rushing around trying to cope with admissions, or lecturing to the students? Or . . .

'Bea? What days does Duncan work here?'

'Let's see? Mondays, Tuesdays and Thursdays, so he'll be coming in tomorrow. Why?'

'Just wondering. What's he like as a doctor?'

'No one better. And what's more his paperwork is none too dusty, which is more than can be said for the other part-timers. You like him, don't you?'

'I think I do.'

'Don't you come coy with me, my girl! You get on like a house on fire. That's about the size of it, isn't it?'

'Yes, I suppose it is.'

'Good!'

It was early evening when Marion joined them at the flat.

Beatrice and Kate had had a siesta, and were feeling more like their old selves, while Stephen had reverted back into a world of his own, his quirky smile implying that he at least was privy to the secrets of the universe, even if he didn't choose to convey them to others.

At first, Marion didn't know how to begin to tell them about Dorothy's suspicions of Lau Peng, but Bea knew her moods too well not to sense that something was worrying her very much indeed.

'Oh, for goodness sake, Marion, stop fiddling with that ridiculous necklace, and spit it out before you do yourself an injury.'

So Marion told them about Lau Peng and the Chinaman in the photograph; adding that Jake had confirmed that the Chinaman was a Communist agent, because he'd been arrested trying to flee the country, so there was no doubt where *his* sympathies lay.

Beatrice and Kate were as shocked by the news as Marion, hotly arguing that just because Lau Peng knew the man, had handed him a book which might or might not have contained instructions or terrorist propaganda, it was no reason to suppose that he was a Communist agent as well.

At this point, Stephen emerged from his dream, making one of those remarks that can be all the more disturbing for appearing to be unimportant. 'He smiles too much!' he announced, opening his eyes and then closing them again; and Kate had a sudden and vivid picture of Lau Peng smiling and smiling, as if the expression has been plastered on like a poster trying to sell a product.

During the discussion, Beatrice grew very quiet, slipping into the kitchen to make yet another cup of tea, though her hand was so shaky that she spilled half of it into the saucers. 'Tell me,' she shouted to Kate and Marion, 'has Jake yet informed the police about his suspicions?' But Marion was quick to reassure her that after much discussion they had decided that it had better be *her* decision, if only because the police would be sure to search the Centre. And then of course, there was the question of Christina . . .

Christina.

The name hung in the air, and all the more potent because they had all so studiously avoided it.

'A bad chooser, that Christina,' Stephen muttered, breaking the spell. 'Like Maudie Cuthbertson, who picked three bounders in a row.'

'Oh, for God's sake!' Beatrice exploded, joining them on the balcony and attacking the dead leaves of a geranium as if her very life depended on it.

'But Lau Peng would *never* do that to Christina. Or to you two for that matter,' Kate stated firmly, trying not to catch Stephen's eyes which were again open and staring at her as if she were half demented.

But to their amazement, Beatrice would have none of it, announcing that a committed Communist wouldn't have qualms about using *anyone*; and adding with more force than Kate would have believed, that they must immediately tell Jake to inform the police.

'But, Bea! Surely we should at least *warn* Christina?' Kate pleaded, wondering at Beatrice's lack of feeling.

Beatrice stood in the doorway of the balcony, her arms crossed and pressed against her, as she stared sightlessly across the city and towards the mainland.

'No. No, I *don't* think so.'

While Christina was returning to the Centre after visiting Lau Peng and a pupil who was sick, the Malay and British Police searched the building, ending in the schoolroom, because the pupils were having a singing lesson and didn't leave until five o'clock.

Marion, Kate and Stephen sat huddled on a bench, while Beatrice sat at the teacher's desk, holding a doll she'd picked up from the floor; and all of them watched every move the policemen made as they searched in things, and under and over and behind them; even ripping open the cover of a cushion, until the room resembled a vast dump of unconnected objects. Books lay with empty jam jars; tipped-up chairs shared the floor with plants disembowelled from their pots; and the map of the world lay like a shroud over a jumble of pencil boxes, and a child's drawing of an angel with a squint.

'We're looking for absolutely anything that might give away Lau Peng's affiliations,' the police chief explained to Beatrice and Stephen. 'And the Centre's where they'll most likely be. You see, we've raided the Chinese quarter so often, that he'd never keep anything incriminating there.'

'Quite,' Beatrice replied, returning to her examination of the doll: lifting its plaits and holding them on top of its head.'

What is she thinking? Marion wondered, watching the tick at the side of Beatrice's eye, which was always a sign that she was reaching the end of her tether. Dear God, hadn't she had enough, without having her world turned upside down yet again?

Marion gazed around the shambles of the room, wondering how many of the pupils were now helping the terrorists or even, God help us, terrorists themselves? But surely none of them could forget *all* that they had been taught? Or did some of them now see the lessons as just another form of brain washing – the conquerors' ways of pacifying with the promise that if they achieved Matriculation, they might be lucky enough to secure a position in the civil service, and what's more with a pension at the end.

What the Hell were they up to now? Marion jumped at the sudden barrage of sound as two of the policemen held a cupboard, while another hit the sides with a truncheon.

And we've been *here* before, Marion reminded herself with some bitterness, thinking of the Japs and their endless searching of the huts; and then later, when they'd thought that at least *that* was behind them, the police searching the first Centre when they'd suspected Joss of buying medicines on the black market.

Marion was reminded of a Chinese proverb that the midwife who had helped with Dorothy's abortion had once quoted. Something about 'If you wish to be happy, never live in interesting times.' In fact, for her money . . .

'No. Not that!'

Stephen was on his feet, shouting at a policeman who was in the act of taking down the photograph of Joss, that hung above the blackboard.

Before she knew what she was doing, Marion was running across the room, her arms outstretched to grab it from him; but as her fingers touched the picture it fell to the ground and shattered, the policeman cursing and telling her not to interfere with their search.

Marion knelt on the floor, carefully picking up the slithers of glass, before turning over the frame and staring at the creased face of Joss, whose expression now appeared to her to be more quizzical than ever. She stared at it for some time, before noticing that the backing had come unstuck at the top and down one side, and that wedged between the photograph and a piece of cardboard were neatly folded papers that seemed to be covered in small Chinese writing.

It's not possible, she told herself. No one would do *that*. Surely no one they knew would use Joss's photograph for such an obscene purpose? To betray . . .

Marion stood up and held the papers out to the chief of police. 'This may be what you are looking for.'

The schoolroom was hushed, everyone watching the man unfold the papers and start to read, first slowly and then quicker and quicker, handing the pages to his assistant as he muttered that they'd got him, they'd really got the little bastard!

No one knew how long Christina had been standing in the doorway, her eyes wide with astonishment as she took in first the chaos and the police, then the abandoned frame, and finally the papers in the police chief's hand.

'*What's happening? What are they doing?*' she cried, staring at each of her friends in turn; but as Marion started towards her, Beatrice let go of the doll and stood up; and with a voice stronger and colder than any of her friends could ever remember, she stated: 'Christina! *We've found you out.*'

Afterwards, no one could be quite sure of the exact sequence in which everything had hapened, except that the police chief had signalled to his men to remain where they were, while Beatrice's voice had continued remorselessly on with her accusations that Christina was in with Lau Peng; that it was *she* who had given the details of the layout of the plantation and Ulrica's arrival; and that she had done so when she had taken over

Beatrice's telephone call to the Centre, and spoken so rapidly to her *fellow communist*, Lau Peng.

Of course, they had all been astonished by her accusations and had protested with vigour; not least Christina, who had shouted at Beatrice, that it was *she* who had saved her life!

'Yes, and that's the thing that's been niggling me ever since,' Beatrice continued in the same icy tone, moving towards Christina as if she might at any moment hit her. 'I may be nearly blind and I don't speak Chinese as you very well know, but when you shouted at that bandit to hold his fire, it wasn't a plea, *it was an order!*'

It was then that Christina had panicked, turning first to Marion and then to Kate, and shouting out that surely they didn't believe what Beatrice was saying? But Marion's face was expressionless, and Kate's full of doubt, as she remembered their arrival at the bungalow, and how Christina had been listening when Dominica had boasted that Teddy had not only guns but a secret store of ammunition.

Again Christina looked at each of her friends in turn: at Marion and then Kate, and then finally at Beatrice, before turning and making a run for the door; but two of the policemen intercepted her, grabbing and holding her tight as she screamed at Beatrice that she should have let the bandit kill her!

No one who was there would ever forget Christina's blazing anger as she struggled to free herself, the policemen pulling her backwards into the passage, while her friends stood in frozen silence as they faced the depths of her betrayal.

It was only when Christina's frenzied shouts had faded, that Beatrice moved, turning on her heels and stumbling out of the room.

Best to keep moving, Beatrice told herself over and over again, groping her way along the passage which was now shadowy and felt strangely chill.

At last she gained the courtyard and started to square

its edges; to walk round it, and then to cross it, and then to walk round it again in the opposite direction. On and on she went, as she tried to avoid the memories that came at her as sharp as bullets, or perhaps as sharp as the one bullet that had lodged in Ulrica's shoulder. Christina taking the telephone receiver to talk to Lau Peng; Christina listening intently to the bandits, not to interpret, but to pass on where Dominica's bedroom was; and above all, Christina as she entered the bungalow behind the bandits, and her ringing voice when she had shouted out to one of them to hold his fire.

This is where we worked together for so long, Beatrice told herself, staring towards the schoolroom window and its welcoming square of light. In that very room, day after day, year after year, Christina had instructed the pupils and the adults on just how to undermine and then to bring death to her father's people. And all because she couldn't forgive them. But for what? Her Scottish name and the legacy her father had bestowed when he'd married a Chinese woman and a half-caste girl had been conceived? Or was it the years of growing up under the white man's rule, when she'd been banned from this place and that; when she'd been forced to learn that if she was to be half-way accepted, it was best to be gentle and inconspicuous. To be *small*.

Beatrice peered up at the sky, where she could just make out a faint peppering of stars; the very same stars that had shone down on them when they had been friends in the camps. Little Christina. Shy, gentle Christina, who above all else had longed to be accepted despite her colour. Aye, there's the rub, thought Beatrice. *Colour*. Colour, that in the first camp had made Sylvia refuse to sleep next to her; colour, that Metro had hinted was not to be trusted; and then the no-colour; the oh-so-white Lieutenant Treeves who had told her he loved her and would wait, and who had then married an oh-so-white nurse.

'We made friends too late,' Beatrice mumbled, dimly aware that she hadn't the strength to walk another step, and sinking on to a bench against the surgery wall.

Or perhaps it hadn't been so much the British, but Yamauchi, the Japanese, who had changed Christina? Perhaps it was he who persuaded her where she should place her allegiance? Who could tell? And what the Hell difference did it make anyway?

Beatrice's head sank slowly on to her folded arms and she slept.

She slept when Kate found her, her specs pushed up into her hair, and one shoe she had kicked off, lying on its side.

'Bea, old love, I've made you some food,' Kate whispered. But Beatrice continued to sleep; so Kate sat by her side, one arm round her friend's shoulders as she picked up the shoe and regarded it thoughtfully.

Such an ordinary shoe, with one lace broken and knotted together; a lace that said everything about the woman who now slept; a woman who had no time, because she had spent her strength trying to help everyone else but herself.

In the end, Beatrice woke with start, jumping up and glaring at Kate as if she'd been sent to spy on her.

'Where the Hell is everyone?'

'Marion's gone. But I've cooked a meal for you and Stephen.'

'I see. So you no longer wish to eat with us, is that it?'

'No. I'm having a snack with Duncan.'

'Then you'd better get on with it, *hadn't you*? And what are you doing with my shoe?'

Beatrice snatched it from Kate's hand, shoving it on her foot and hurrying into the Centre as she flung over her shoulder that she was still just about able to cook a meal, or did they think she was even incapable of *that*?

Beatrice's bad temper continued throughout supper, until Stephen, who had felt very sorry for her, lashed out that he was fed up with being her whipping boy, and why didn't she take her anger out on her so-called friend? At which Beatrice had another of her swift changes of mood, nodding her head in agreement and sinking into the armchair that Christina had given her as a house-warming present when they had first moved into the flat.

'Stephen, have you thought that it's as if the whole of the last five years have been for nothing? We've let Joss down completely, you do realise that – allowing it to happen right under our very noses. How they must have laughed! The mole and the matchstick! A blind old woman kidding herself she was on top of things, *and as for you*! At least *you've* got your eyes. Couldn't you have seen what Christina and Lau Peng were up to, you bungling old fool?'

Beatrice hit the arm of the chair with her fist, as if it was just as much to blame as the giver; before turning away with a look of such defeat that Stephen eased himself out of his chair and went to her. Gently, he laid his hand on a shoulder, which was neither as broad nor as strong as he had believed; and the knowledge made him feel a man once again, if only that Beatrice so obviously needed him.

'Bea? Isn't it time we went home?'

'You'd hate to go back,' Bea mumbled, turning her head even further away from his stare.

'I dunno. Wouldn't mind seeing the old place again.'

Stephen drew himself up, buttoning the top of his pyjamas because it was important to be formally dressed. 'If I've got to die, might as well be on the National Health.'

Beatrice heard his voice, but it was some seconds before she understood what he was saying; and when she did, she looked up and saw that her sparring partner was a very proud old man who wanted none of her damned sympathy thank you.

'You old so-and-so! You might have told me you knew.'

'And spoil your game? Oh no, Monica, I couldn't deprive . . .'

'For the hundredth time, *it is Beatrice*.'

Stephen ran his hand through his beautiful hair and

smiled the secret smile that she knew so well. 'Monica, Joss, Beatrice. What's the difference? Just three bossy females bent on making my life Hell!'

They looked at each other and grinned; Stephen taking a peppermint out of his pocket, and offering it in just the same way as he'd done to his first love at the age of five. And Beatrice accepted it in the same off-hand manner as the little girl who had introduced him to the game of Doctors and Nurses, and who had been so very bossy and argumentative.

Kate stood outside the door of the flat for some time, before she managed to gather enough courage to enter. She even waited outside the sitting room door; but when she knocked and went in, her words tumbled out so fast, that Beatrice had no chance of interrupting.

'I'm sorry, Bea, I really am, but I can't go on with my studies. And I've been meaning to tell you for some time, and I know what you're going to say, but my mind's made up because I can't stand medical school a day longer, and I want to come back, and I want to come back *now* when I'm needed, and I've talked it over with Duncan – he's waiting downstairs – and he says he'd be happy to help me settle in, and I'd be doing something I really wanted, and all those years of studying won't be wasted, and please, *please* try and understand, because the last thing I'd ever want is to feel that I've let you down.'

As an afterthought, and because she was out of breath, Kate turned to Stephen and asked him if *he* would mind her being around; but Stephen pointed to Beatrice, informing her that she had better ask The Governor.

'Well!' said Beatrice, knocked out by a revelation which had come so fast on the heels of the first. 'Well!' she repeated, Kate staring in such an agony of suspense, that all she could think of was to say 'Well!' yet again.

It was Stephen who broke the tension, telling Beatrice to pull herself together, and to stop sounding like some

Victorian melodrama that was trying to hold the audience in suspense.

After much discussion, and though Bea was deeply upset by Kate's decision, she finally accepted it with the best grace she could muster; especially when Stephen hissed that it couldn't have come at a better time!

'What time?' demanded Kate. So they told her how they were thinking that they'd both like to return to London; and Kate was so thrilled by the idea that she *really* might be needed, that she rushed out and dragged Duncan up to the flat, telling him that if he didn't help at the Centre full-time she would never speak to him, ever again!

It was midnight when they opened a bottle of brandy that Stephen had kept hidden, and which he'd managed to salvage from Raffles before the Japanese invasion. 'And if you tell me I can't have any,' he informed Beatrice, waving his arms, 'then I'll blow the gaff on the time your bloomers fell down in the middle of a Government House reception!'

The friends sat round the table, all that had happened that day washed from their minds by an exhaustion that forced them to accept the past for what it was: gone. So they talked of the future, and then they talked of the future again; until finally they said goodnight with the first pale streaks of the dawn.

The same dawn that crept between the bars of a cell, where Christina lay on her back staring at the cracks in the ceiling.

10
Singapore

Ulrica was delighted that Sister Briggs had given her a bed in the corner, though she couldn't decide whether it was because she was a nun, or because she considered her a difficult patient.

Really, sometimes the British could try the patience of a saint what with their hearty Good Mornings at dawn, and their 'Have you slept well?' when they knew she hadn't dozed off until 4 a.m. and they'd been the ones to wake her!

Ulrica smoothed the sheet and tried to compose herself, but her feet were cramped because of the tight way they had tucked her in, and was it not enough that the top part of her was all strapped up, without making her feel as if the bottom part of her was bound as well.

You are a most ungrateful woman, Ulrica told herself severely, choosing a grape from an enormous bunch that Dorothy had brought in, together with a pretty bedjacket that was far too young and frivolous for a nun, and which she adored.

After a strenuous ten minutes of praying, Ulrica managed to compose herself; and that, despite the cleaners moving her bed and jogging her shoulder not once but twice. Still, she *was* making progress, and if her prayers for them were more diligent than loving, she would try to do better the next time.

'Dear God from whom all wisdom and love flows, watch over my little Dorothy and give her that peace of mind that will bring her the serenity for which she searches.'

Dear, dear Dorothy, what a devoted child she was, and how very like her to feel guilty because she had remained in Singapore. As if she could have done anything to stop the bullet! Besides, it was important that she should get to know Jake Haulter, who was not half as crooked as he liked to make out.

Ulrica regarded her fingers, which were sticky from the marmalade a nurse had insisted in spreading on her toast, when she would much have preferred it plain. Still, if it gave them pleasure . . . She tried to reach her flannel but it was too painful, so she sucked her fingers as she brooded on the amazing diversity of God's creations.

There was much good in Jake, of that she was sure. It was only that he *would* do things despite himself. And then, when he felt that uneasiness which always came from going against one's better nature, he stifled it by kicking up his heels even higher, in exactly the same stubborn manner as her younger brother! Men! They were all the same; even Father Joseph, who saw himself as a stern upholder of God's law, when really he was as soft as the butter he would insist on denying himself. No, Jake was a good match for Dorothy, and she for him; and oh how superior they would be together because they would be so certain that they were outside the rules, when of course they were just the same as everyone else, except that they questioned the Whys and Wherefores which, come to think of it, was no bad thing! Besides, they were children and like children would have to make their own mistakes until one day . . . One day they would be grown up enough to admit that they needed each other, and then the Good Lord would be given the chance to enter their lives and to bless them.

Ulrica spent the next ten minutes contemplating God's love and making a list before the priest visited her for confession. 1) She had committed the sin of pride, for had she not boasted that she was proud of the way she had driven to the plantation? 2) She had allowed hate to enter her soul when the bandits had lined them up in the sun. After all, they had only done what they believed was right for the good of *their* country, and if they also believed that the means justified the ends, who was she to condemn anyone when she was such a sinner herself? 3) After the kindness of Metro in sending her that gigantic bouquet, it was *most* ungrateful that she had thought it was rather embarrassing. How could any of God's flowers be embarrassing, even the overblown roses that had to be grown under special conditions and were denied the full glory of God's good air. And then there was 4) Christina. Could God ever forgive her for the anger she had felt at the child's betrayal, when she now saw that she might have been able to help her? How very typical of her blindness, that she had rushed off to help the lepers, when there was someone under her own arrogant nose who had so much need of her. Poor Christina, and poor all the other half-castes who had been born out of colonisation, and had then been rejected as if they didn't belong and the Europeans did. No, she would need a long time with the priest, if she was to cleanse her soul and receive God's forgiveness – even of the sin of thinking that the hospital priest was a poor substitute for Father Joseph; and had probably been given the job because of his bad breath, under the misguided assumption that the sick would be too ill to notice.

Ulrica bent her head and prayed, until at last she came to that peace she had been striving for all morning. Indeed, even when she was served macaroni cheese, she accepted it with a smile, making quite sure that the nurses weren't looking, before wrapping it in a piece of strong paper.

At the moment when Ulrica was hiding her lunch, Dorothy was sitting in Raffles bar with Maggie, who was telling her for the umpteenth time how much she missed Jim and the kids; and how, if she was honest, she had been narked about Dorothy and Jake getting together, because of her fling with Jake when they had first been liberated.

'After all, Dot, why shouldn't you have a holiday romance?'

Dorothy wondered whether to tell Maggie, and then decided she might as well because she'd find out soon enough. 'It's not just a holiday romance. He's coming over for Christmas, and then we'll play it by ear.'

The moment she said it, Dorothy knew she'd have been better to keep her mouth shut, because Maggie launched into a lecture about how it was time that they both settled down, and that if Dorothy wanted to start a family she'd better get a move on.

Christ, Dorothy thought, why is it that the moment anyone gets married and starts having kids, they want the whole bloody world to do the same? Well, the same I am not! Have a family? That was a joke. Hadn't she already had one, or was little Violet and the tiny slither of life she'd spewed into a bucket, something different? No, she and Jake would only ever have themselves. For one thing, they were too selfish. And besides, if she was as honest as Ulrica was always saying, then they'd taken enough risks in their lives without having to add to them.

Oh no. Not another little mummy!

Dorothy watched Marion with some distaste, as she came towards them, smiling that charming smile that was altogether too tentative considering she knew damned well that everyone liked her. And when Marion told them that it wasn't just Lau Peng who'd been Communist but Christina as well, it crossed Dorothy's mind that there was another one who'd been oh so charming; and if she'd known what a ruthless cow Christina really was, she might have had a bit more time for her.

'Remember in our second camp when Rose and Bernard were caught?'

Marion lifted her voice, as if she knew that Dorothy

was miles away; and because Dorothy had *not* wished her thoughts to be interrupted, it pleased her to remind Marion that it had been *her* chum, Lillian, who had informed on the two of them.

But Marion didn't appear to notice. 'Do you remember how people suspected Christina at first, and how hurt and angry she was that we hadn't trusted her?'

'Well, this time we did trust her,' Dorothy reminded Marion. 'And just look where it got us!'

Marion was quite aware of her affect on Dorothy and even knew why, so she made her excuses and left to go up to her room. However, she bumped into Alice in the passage, and her heart lifted when she saw that at least *she* looked pleased to see her.

'Marion, I'm so glad I've caught you. I wanted to let you know that I shan't be going home, because I've decided to stay on a bit longer. You see Kate's got to go back to Australia to sort things out, and Beatrice said she could do with a hand!'

'Alice, it sounds an excellent idea, it really does. But what about your father?'

'It's my life,' Alice told her, with some force. 'I'm going to ring him tonight, and perhaps you wouldn't mind having a word with him, when you get back?'

'Of course.'

Marion could hardly believe that Alice was the same girl who had been so nervous when they had met at the airport. How incredible, that in such a short time she had somehow solved her problems, and that now she could remember her mother in camp, and in that remembering had come to terms with the past.

'Marion, I'm glad I came in spite of everything.'

'So am I.'

As Marion said it, she knew it was true. But why for her? What had happened since they'd come to Singapore, that had given her this new lease of life? This extraordinary feeling, that when she woke in the morning, she no longer needed to drag herself through the day, because she might even enjoy it?

Again Marion congratulated Alice on her decision, before almost running to her room, because she wanted to write to Ben and tell him all about it. But when she took up her pen, she found that she couldn't, so she ordered a gin sling to have with her bath.

'Let there be you, let there be me, let there be oysters under the sea,' sang Marion, because she knew she was letting go of Ben; that she didn't need to explain herself any longer, not to anyone! For too long she'd been hanging on to the memory of Clifford, to the thought of his new baby, and to her so-called responsibility to their son. Well, Ben could very well look after himself. In fact the next time he got into debt, bless him, he'd have to bail himself out and a good thing too!

'What I am going to do,' she announced to the taps, fitting her big toe into one of them, 'is to buy a whole new wardrobe. Nothing practical of course, but frivolous little numbers to go with my new state of mind, and to Hell with the bank manager.' Having decided her course for the afternoon, Marion lathered her hands and made an 'O' with her thumb and finger, blowing bubbles at the ceiling and taking much pleasure in bursting them as they floated down.

Three hours later, Marion staggered into Raffles carrying an armful of shopping: three dresses, a ridiculous hat of pink straw, and two pairs of sandals; and if she now felt guilty at how much she had spent she also had the strength of mind not to blank it out with a drink, and instead decided to drop in on Beatrice and Kate because happiness needed to be shared.

'If there's one thing gets up my nose, it's the high-handed way of officials,' Bea explained to Kate, as she unwrapped the new frame for Joss's photograph.

'Don't I know,' Kate smiled, thinking of their visit to the police who had taken Joss's photograph as some kind of evidence.

'Honestly,' she had told Duncan later, 'Bea's the cat's whiskers when it comes to a battle. And that *poor* man, how he had stood it when Bea railed on about how they bloody well knew whose finger prints were on it, and were they trying to outdo the Sewage Department in their deliberate simplemindedness, considering Christina had confessed to being a Communist, up hill and down dale?'

Beatrice placed Joss's photograph in the frame, inserting the back and making quite sure that it was secure because she didn't want the humidity to get inside and spoil it.

She lifted the picture and hung it on the nail, before both of them stepped back and inspected their friend.

'There,' said Kate. 'Fighting fit again.'

'Yes. And Kate? She'd be awfully bucked to know *you're* taking over.'

'But you, Bea? You're not too disappointed in me?'

'I shall still be handing on the torch – just a different one, that's all, and you can always resume your training later on.'

'That's what Duncan said.'

Ah! I knew Duncan would creep into the conversation somewhere, Beatrice told herself, thinking what a great support he would be for Kate, and that if she'd tried she couldn't have thought of anyone more suitable, and not just for Kate but for the Centre.

'Tell you one good thing that's come out of this,' Beatrice said, as she adjusted Joss's picture first to the right and then to the left and then back again. 'Never realised we had so many friends. Honestly, offers of help have been flooding in, ever since they heard about Christina and Lau Peng.'

'Bea, what'll happen to Christina?'

'Who knows?'

Christina was wondering the same thing as she lay on the bed in her cell in Changi prison.

Not that she regretted what she had done, for wasn't it for The Cause; though the sight of Ulrica lying on the ground would stay with her until her dying day. Still, the innocent were always the casualties of war, and not least when the war was just.

She sat up and stared at the bare wall of her cell, where two flies were climbing and interlocking, before going their separate ways. So how were they treating Lau Peng, she wondered, turning her head and staring at the sky between the bars. Not that *she* had any complaints, but then she was just as much a soldier as any of the comrades in the jungle; and soldiers learnt to take what was coming, or so her father had always said.

No, not 'Father'; that was the middle-class word. 'Daddy' was what she had called him. Her Daddy from Scotland, for it always helped when she thought of him as being not quite British, because after all Scotland had been conquered by the enemy which was the real British south of the border; and his ancestors as well as her mother's had been forced to bow under their yoke.

Christina sighed. Now she would never see his country, or her Gran in the house overlooking the harbour and the fishing boats that brought in the herrings. Gran Mary Campbell, who was now eighty-two, and who still wrote to her on her birthday and at Christmas. 'Remember, Pet, always be a good girl and say your prayers. From your ever loving Gran, Mary Elizabeth.' There would be no more letters ending like that, when she heard what her grandchild had done. *Not that she cared.* The past was the past, to be packed away once the country was theirs, and they could go into the bright future, shoulder to shoulder with their loyal comrades in arms!

Christina smiled as she remembered the Communist poster they had printed and which was to be distributed underground. 'Unite comrades, against the Capitalist White Aggressor' it had begun, and ended with the uplifting slogan: 'He who believes is invincible!'

And also '*She*'!

Christina squared her shoulders, and if it took some discipline not to think of her friends or wonder what they were thinking of her, it was a small price to pay for a future in which she would be a member of the Executive.

Christina faced the door as she heard footsteps in the passage; footsteps that stopped when the guard turned the key in the lock, and Marion's voice said 'Thank you'.

'I said I wanted no visitors,' Christina flung at the guard as he and Marion entered. 'I suppose, Marion, you pulled strings? After all, it's always so easy for you British!'

Afterwards, Christina couldn't remember all that had been said, except that she had become more and more angry, and that had helped her to reject all that Marion and her friends still believed with such stupid conviction. How dare she have suggested that they should wait for Independence to be given, when on *their* terms the Chinese would still be third-class citizens; and how dare she condescend in offering her her 'forgiveness'. Marion was in no position to forgive, because it was she, Christina, who had been offended against, ever since the day she was born.

A thought which she tried to censor cut through her defences: the three of them, Bea, Stephen and herself, wandering around the new Centre and marvelling at what they could achieve in such a splendid place. All the plans they had had and how glowing they had been on that first day before she had seen the light.

But what had made her most angry of all was Marion's suggestion that she should co-operate with the authorities, so that she might be sent to a rehabilitation camp instead of another prison. Didn't she know the glory of suffering for a Cause, and the knowledge that your comrades outside were speaking your name with pride?

Indeed, one day there would be a statue to her. 'Christina Campbell, whose heroism helped to lay the foundation stone of our state.'

Despite herself, a doubt entered Christina's mind. What about the many heroines in camp? Blanche, whose courageous death still had the power to hurt. Brave, prickly Blanche, who had so hated the class system, and who had used the Japs for her own ends. Where was *she* now, and where was the statue to her and all the hundreds of others? Nowhere! Nor would there ever be, given the shame of what they stood for. Still, at least she, Christina, was carrying on the class struggle!

Christina was well aware that she was justifying herself, but she didn't care. All she had to do was hang on to it all: the teachings, the dialectic view of history, the knowledge that all workers would one day unite in their struggle for a place in the sun; and damn Marion and those big kind eyes, and her look of pain when she had flung at her that it was not Lau Peng who had recruited her, but *she* who had recruited Lau Peng! Oh, that had been the most glorious moment of revenge.

That night Christina refused supper, and if the guard had been white she would have knocked it into his face.

Even when she sank on to the hard bed, she still retained traces of her anger, and it was a long time before she drifted into a sleep bedevilled by dreams . . .

They were all having such a good time: Blanche, Rose, Joss, little Susie and Debbie; and all of them from the hut, running up and down the beach and throwing a ball that grew larger and larger until none of them was able to hold it. And still it grew larger, until it burst into a great roaring laugh that spread out and over them; and they were all laughing and smiling together, because they loved each other, and the day would go on for ever.

It was the final dream before Christina awoke to the sound of the key turning in the lock of her cell. But then dreams are no respecters of ideology, even when the dreamer had committed the whole of herself to its values.

11
Singapore

'I feel on top of the world!' Ulrica announced, for today Sister Briggs had allowed her to sit in a chair! And not only that, for she had had a surprise visit from Father Joseph, who had rushed in between visits to the Bishop and the Cashin garage that had a much-needed spare part for Sister Anna.

Not that the visit hadn't had its embarrassing moments, for Father Joseph had always had a tendency to drop things and could be very clumsy with inanimate objects, especially chairs. And then there was the question of his entrance. 'So that's where you've been hiding yourself,' he had bellowed, almost trampling the almoner in his rush to her side, as he had demanded to know how his good friend was getting on, before launching into news of the Mission. Of course it was unfortunate that he had illustrated the items with such graphic movements, for Sister Briggs had been forced to desert her sterilizing unit, so as to remove the vase from behind his head.

Still, on the whole it had been a most stimulating day and she couldn't wait to get back into harness, especially after Father Joseph's hints that Sister Mary was planning a campaign to cancel her arrangements for a school in one of the villages.

Then too, it had been a happy coincidence that Beatrice had dropped in just as Father Joseph was thinking of leaving. How they had taken to each other! Especially when they'd discovered their mutual distrust of authority, Bea riding her hobby horse of the iniquities of the Sewage Department, while Father Joseph had outdone her with his lecture on the Government's mix-ups over re-settlement, *especially* housing; ending with his pulling some building plans out of his cassock, together with other items he happened to have in the same pocket: pencils, clips, bits of string, a bag of peanuts, and for some reason a mask of Micky Mouse. In fact, if it had not hurt her so much, she would have joined in the laughter as her two friends scrambled around her chair on all fours, Sister Briggs standing over them and announcing that she'd never in all her born days witnessed such a diabolical shambles, and *that* included the night the circus had accompanied a high wire artist right into casualty!

After Father Joseph had at last gathered his things together and left, Ulrica and Beatrice had a long discussion about the Centre and their friends; especially the plight of Christina, which was not helped by her continual refusal to co-operate with the authorities.

Dear Bea, how very angry and yet concerned she had been about Christina, for she had now convinced herself that someone had 'Got at her', and that if only someone else could get at her – only more so – she would immediately see the error of her ways and repent.

It took an atheist, thought Sister Ulrica, to have such a blind faith in words, which after all had not been given by God, but by man, and could be twisted to represent anything, if only you put your mind to it.

Still, at least she'd been able to reassure Beatrice that after she and Stephen had left for England, she would visit Christina in jail; and if she was not able to convert her, then at least she could offer the hand of friendship.

And so the circle completes itself, Ulrica mused, thinking of Yamauchi, and how she had visited *him* in the very same jail. Poor misguided man. Yet another victim of the belief in words from above; but then any rules that were laid down to twist the human spirit were meant to be broken, and that was what neither he nor Christina could ever accept.

Ulrica became aware that her shoulder was painful, but she was determined that she would stay in the chair as long as she was allowed, for was it not part of her penance, just as the shot in her shoulder was God's reminder of her mortality? She reached for the cross that hung from her neck, thanking the Good Lord, that within His laws *all* could travel their natural path and be blessed; even such a sinner as herself who had refused a guard for her truck, and who must bear responsibility for much of that terrible day.

Oh Blessed Lord, guide your sinner and her dear friends in the paths of righteousness.

Dear Beatrice, how serene she had looked now that she knew that the Centre would be in the safe hands of Kate and Duncan, and that when she returned to England, she and Stephen would be living with Marion. Not that she didn't have misgivings, for that was her way. Still, at least she'd been persuaded that it would be as good for Marion as herself, if only because of Marion's deep need to look after people. Not that it hadn't been very stupid of her to use the expression 'Look after', for Bea had bridled immediately. But as she had pointed out: those who look after people, also need to be looked after; and Marion's loneliness had been as transparent as the pain of her divorce – despite her protests that it had all been friendly. 'Friendly!' How could a separation be described by a word that meant coming together? It was absurd!

And Stephen? What was it Beatrice had told her with such enthusiasm . . .

Ulrica dozed for a moment and then woke with a start. Of course! Marion planned to turn her study into a bedsitting room, so that when Stephen grew too weak, he could lie and look out at the garden, his two bossy females waiting on him hand and foot, while pretending to thwart him at every turn. And when at last the Good

Lord gathered him to Himself, Monica and Joss would be waiting in that Heaven where one day they would all be united.

Again Ulrica nodded, and then slept; and Sister Briggs, who happened to be passing with a bedpan, tucked a pillow behind her head and ticked off a second year for making such an appalling din.

Beatrice had had one heck of a morning, what with writing to various medical authorities in London to ask what openings there were for her expertise in tropical diseases, or even if there was a possibility that she might lecture. And then, on top of everything else, Stephen had mislaid his one good suit which had turned up at the bottom of his laundry basket and covered in mould! In the end, she had had to wash it and pray it would dry in time for the farewells, which of course it hadn't, poor Kate having to iron it over and over, while Stephen had wandered about getting under their feet, until she had been forced to remove him bodily. The man was a positive danger, and what's more not only to himself but to everyone else.

Now, she and Stephen and Alice and Kate were jammed into Jake's car, the man driving like a maniac to the airport, and all because he'd been delayed by some devious deal or other. Typical!

'Jake! If you don't slow down this instant, I shall be forced to fling myself out, if only to save my life.'

Jake grinned, telling Bea to hold on to her hat, for he was determined to get to the airport in time to say goodbye to Dorothy, Marion and Maggie. Especially Dorothy.

'So tell me, Kate,' Jake shouted over his shoulder. 'How long will you be in Australia before you come back to take over?'

'As short a time as possible! And Jake? *Promise* you'll make sure that Bea and Stephen do some packing, because I'll have no time if the take-over's to be done at all.'

'*I* shan't be doing any packing,' Stephen announced, waving to a bartender whom he had once known extremely well. 'I will be buying an entire wardrobe: a suit or two from Savile Row, one or two pairs of shoes from Lobbs, a titfer from Locks, and a positive drawerful of shirts.'

'Oh yes? And where, might I ask, will you get the where-with-all?' Bea enquired in her most sarcastic tone.

'From my deadly dull sister, under the threat that if she doesn't cough up I'll plonk myself down in her bungalow! After all, a man needs to look decent when visiting his club, especially when he hasn't darkened its doors since that row with Maudie Cuthbertson's better half.'

They were saved from a blow by blow account, by Jake screeching to a stop and heaving them all out, before throwing the keys at Kate and shouting to lock up the car, as he ran into the airport and almost knocked Dorothy down with the force of his embrace.

'God, I thought I'd missed you.'

'Will you, Jake? Miss me, I mean?'

'Just occasionally. And you be sure to go and see Harry Forrest and ask about my selling his Daimler. Only I've just heard it's definite he won't be coming back.'

'So that's why you rushed to get here.' Over his shoulder, Dorothy noticed that some of the passengers for London were already queuing at the exit.

'Till Christmas, Jake. And don't forget you're bringing out more ivory. And you might sniff around for some good jade while you're about it.'

'Right, Miss Bossy Boots.'

'And by the by, what about the reward money? After all, you must be due for quite a wack.'

Jake let go of Dorothy's hand and lighted a cigarette, and it crossed her mind that he was embarrassed. 'Thought I'd donate it to the Centre,' he mumbled, looking down at her and then winking. 'After all, I've got myself a rich widow, so now I can afford to be generous!'

Marion and Beatrice had found an empty bench so that Stephen could sit, because the crowd seemed to have an electrifying effect on him, for he was shifting about as if at any moment he might get up and dance.

'Well, Bea? It's been an odd sort of a reunion.'

Bea made that moue of her mouth that was so typical: half bitter and half amused. 'Hardly what we'd anticipated.'

'No.' Marion stood up, putting her arms round Beatrice, and saying that she'd see them both at Christmas, before turning to Stephen and kissing him on both cheeks.

It was at this moment that a familiar voice managed to make itself heard above the babble of voices.

'Coooeee!'

Elbowing through the crowd and overdressed as usual came Dominica, beaming from ear to ear; and even when she heard Stephen's remark that it was that ghastly female again, her smile didn't so much as falter, as she informed them that she had news of the greatest importance to impart! She had *not* come to say au revoir, for after the terrible business up-country, she and Teddy had decided to come to England the very next month! So they had not seen the last of her!

After much exclaiming, it was Alice who pointed out that except for Kate and Sister Ulrica, they would all be in England for Christmas!

'That settles it,' Marion announced triumphantly. 'You must all come to me for the day!' And as she said it, she remembered the years of internment when they'd kept up their spirits by telling each other that they'd all be home by Christmas. And now it seemed it was really going to happen.

The plane gathered its strength like a cat: the engines roaring until the whole structure shook, before it finally taxied forward and lifted into the air; where it turned, its starboard towards the city of Singapore that lay as bright as a box of bricks, and enclosed by the blue of the South China Sea.

Onwards it soared, skirting the secret jungle that wrapped the land in its impenetrable roof of green.

And in the wake of the plane's roar, the birds and the animals and the insects settled once again to their business of searching and devouring, dying and giving birth; but above all avoiding the predatory beasts of the earth. Especially man.

12
London

That winter it snowed, the flakes whirling over the city, and so light that the slightest movement of air shifted their weight: one moment piling them against the buildings, and the next, dispersing them so that they fanned out across the highways and pavements, and all the sounds of the city were deadened; and everything, even the mean streets of the East End, were changed into an unfamiliar and magical landscape.

Even Maggie and Jim's house was transformed, the lights in the narrow windows seeming like the cutouts in a lantern; while in the yard behind, the rounded figure of Blanche – scarf over coat over cardigan over jersey – hardened the snow between her gloves, before adding it to the tipsy snowman who sported her father's cap. She was singing 'One Man Went to Mow', just as her mother had sung it in camp, and if her namesake could have seen her, she would have noticed the rebellious gleam in her eye.

No. She was *not* going to wear her party frock to Auntie Marion's. She was going to wear the red with the squiggly bits that Mum had got her on holiday. '*I won't!*' she screamed at the window, sticking her tongue out at her brother who had climbed up on to the chair and was swinging on the curtain; the condensation turning him into a strange underwater creature that shifted and slid behind the glass. Then, he was lifted bodily and propped on the hip of his mother, who's mouth opened and closed in anger, and the child not at all afraid, but pushing his finger between her teeth.

In Church Street, Kensington, a lorry slowly made its way up the hill, the man in the back shovelling grit out on to the road, where the snow was impacted and blackened by Christmas traffic.

As it passed the Bennett Antiques, a scattering of grit ricocheted against a window that displayed vases and figurines from the East, plus a notice which announced that a selection of jade and ivory could be viewed within.

It was very cold in the shop, and the black and white cat stirred itself and stretched, leaping on to the ledge and through the bars of the back window, and on to the roof of the store room. Here it paused, picking its way across the covering of snow and through a crack in the landing window, where it sat for a moment, its tongue fastidiously searching out the dirt between its claws, before streaking up the stairs and into the warmth of the front room.

Jake and Dorothy sat side by side totting up the profits, every now and then pouring themselves a drink or picking from a plate of smoked salmon and thin slices of brown bread and butter, which Jake had fetched from Jackson's. While behind them, on an inlaid table, lay a pile of festively wrapped presents that had caused much heart-searching: not too expensive because that would send Maggie into one of her Bolshie moods, but still amusing enough to surprise and delight.

In the two months since their arrival in London, Dorothy had put on weight – indeed she was almost voluptuous – while Jake was even slimmer. Or perhaps he only appeared slimmer, because of the new suit from Harrods whose cost would be lost in the office expenses. But then, both Dorothy and Jake would always live above their own or anyone else's income, because the scramble for money was part of its charm; that, and the security it gave them against a world that had always misused their talents in order to keep its own hands pristine.

Dorothy pushed her chair back and stretched. 'That's it for the day, so why don't we go the Odeon and take in a flick?'

'Why not?' Jake eased down his tie and grinned at his rich and indulgent widow. 'And if the car won't start we can always walk.' But they knew they were far too lazy to do any such thing; that they would stop at the first pub and have a drink and a sandwich, because for the first time in their lives they didn't have to do anything that they didn't want to.

On the other side of Hyde Park, in a street named after Charles the Second, a street where the residents were not only rich but also respectable, was the house of a Mr Richard Courtenay, who was trying to concentrate on the *Telegraph* crossword, which he was convinced was twice as difficult as usual.

He had certainly lost weight, but then he was very concerned about his daughter, who had not only stayed out East long after her friends had returned, but when she *had* come back, had displayed a new and uncalled-for wilfulness, which had reminded him of his wife before he had taken her so firmly in hand.

Only the day before, Alice had threatened that if she didn't get a place of her own, she would cash in the shares of her mother's legacy and go on a trip round the world – or anyway as least as far as Malaya. Really, he didn't know what the younger generation was coming to, what with their passion for this negro jazz and the terrible muck they plastered all over their faces.

Mr Courtenay lowered the paper and regarded his daughter, who was curled up in front of the fire, reading. One thing was sure, he'd lost his sweet little girl, and if he didn't watch out, those interfering women from the camps would take her over lock, stock and barrel!

Alice was aware of his scrutiny and looked up, smiling

at her father, who was damned if he was going to smile back.

Poor Daddy, always anticipating the worst and not realising that she *did* love him, even if he was an old fuddy duddy; and for goodness' sake, she was only moving to Maida Vale, not to the ends of the earth.

Alice poked the fire until it blazed, before returning to her detective story, though it was difficult to concentrate because of her father's sighs as he turned to the business page, which could still be relied on to confirm all of his deepest misgivings.

On the slopes of Primrose Hill, a pack of dogs tore through the laurel bushes, the snow showering on to their coats and into the imprints of their paws; while across the road, the roar of wild animals rose from the Regent's Park Zoo: lions, tigers, elephants and hyenas, pacing the fastness of their cages as they glared longingly at the freedom of paths now empty of visitors.

Higher up on the same hill, the house of Mrs Marion Jefferson was in a turmoil of activity: Beatrice in the kitchen making bread as it should be made: the North Country way and none of your muck from the shops; while in the drawing room, Stephen desperately tried to unravel the tinsel, which seemed to keep re-knotting itself until it was in a worse muddle than when he had started. Still, he was comforted by the sound of Marion muttering angrily as she tried to pull out the leaves of the table, which hadn't been done since Ben was small and they'd had a fancy dress party before he was sent off to prep school.

Honestly, they'd never be ready by Christmas, not in a thousand years, what with the stuffing to make for the turkey – two varieties, one for each end – and the mountain of sprouts to be prepared, to say nothing of her Christmas presents which were still in their shop bags and hidden on top of the wardrobe. Marion paused to scratch off a droplet of wax with her nail, trying to recall whether the table has been a wedding or anniversary present, and brooding on the complex nature of Bea: so adult about most things, but who had taken to wandering into her bedroom and peering about her as if searching for something, and in just the same way as Ben had done as a boy. One thing was certain, Bea's present had better be good!

It had been Ben's idea to get her a typewriter; because, as he'd pointed out, once Bea had learnt to touch-type it would be much easier for her to write up her lectures, and then there was the book she was thinking of starting: 'A Practical Guide to the More Common Tropical Diseases'; for she had not forgotten or indeed forgiven Kate for handing over her own and that bloody French doctor's notes, *and* to the first medic she happened to run into once they'd been freed.

Marion had to admit that she too had been surprised, for the notes had cost both the women long hours of writing in secret; or, when Bea's eyes had become too bad, dictating her observations to Kate.

Marion fetched her best and largest tablecloth and shook it out, sighing as she remembered the disastrous party she had given so that Stephen and Bea could be introduced to her friends, and one of them back from Paris had happened to remark that French doctors were better than any other.

'*Better!*' Bea had spluttered, flakes of cheese biscuit spraying out of her mouth. 'What do you mean, "Better"? "Better" as in cold as cods; or "better" as in taking notes while some poor patient is dying at their elbow? Well as far as *I'm* concerned, *never* is the answer to that. Not on your Nellie or any other part of your person!' With which statement she had blundered out and into her room, where she had comforted herself by putting on her new record of 'Nymphs and Shepherds', quite oblivious to the fact that the windows were open and the guests couldn't hear themselves complain.

There was a loud kick at the door as the subject to Marion's thoughts stormed into the room, hands held high and covered in flour, which had also scattered itself across her Fair Isle jersey and up the side of her face.

'That bloody oven. It couldn't cook books let alone bread!'

'Look, Bea, I *told* you. There's a perfectly splendid baker in Camden Town, and what's more he bakes all the bread himself, *and* from his own recipe.'

'And bunged full of chemicals, I don't doubt. Well you can kill your guests if you wish, but you're not about to knock me off!'

With which statement, Bea stamped out and into the drawing room, letting fly at Stephen because she was quite sure he was pinching her bullseyes.

'And what the Hell are you doing with that tinsel?'

'What do you think I'm doing? Knitting?'

Marion fetched the glasses, holding each to the light before setting it on the table, and deciding that Stephen's present of a typing course was purely from self-interest; for he had happened to let drop that the pubs would be open at exactly the same time as Bea's lessons.

A scruffy band of choir boys turned the corner into the road, their rear brought up by the vicar, who was longing for his tea and the homemade jam his sister had sent him.

Good King Wenceslas looked out on the feast of
  Stephen,
When the snow lay round about, deep and crisp
  and even.

The singing was as pure as the singers were not, the smallest and scruffiest rattling a collection box as he stared up at the lighted windows, from which three faces stared back at him: Bea frowning because the carol moved her and she didn't hold with all that nonsense; Stephen muttering a ruder version he'd learnt in the trenches of France; and Marion thinking of the Christmas when Ben had woken her singing the very same words, his hands and face covered in chocolate and peanut butter.

Beyond the city, the countryside humped and dipped under its weight of snow, the vales of Yorkshire seeming as secretive as its inhabitants, who always cut out the 'buts' and the 'thes' of their speech, so as not to give more away than they must.

From a barracks of a house between Pickering and York emerged the reluctant figure of Dominica and her elderly host, dear Teddy's uncle.

Of course the man was mad, she told herself, wrapping her fur coat even tighter around her, as he explained that when the English said something was 'Not bad,' they really meant that it was quite good; and very often a 'Bloody marvellous' – pardon the expression – could mean the opposite, don't you know.

'Come along, Dodo, best foot forward and you'll see, you'll be as hot as toast when we return. Question of pepping up the circulation and all the gubbins.' The uncle strode ahead, every now and then stopping and shouting encouragingly that she'd get the swing of things after a few more miles.

Really, thought Dominica, if the world believes that the East is mysterious, then they should just try Yorkshire! Still, at least she wouldn't be shot at, though even that was a possibility; for hadn't the uncle marched her into a wood with a gun slung under his arm, explaining that if she didn't stay in line, her situpon would most likely be peppered by shot!

'Dear God, deliver me from this freezing climate,' prayed Dominica, comforting herself with the thought of her new wardrobe, because in this hellish cold she'd had to have a new everything, including her first fur coat. Never mind, tonight she and dear Teddy would be returning to civilisation, and tomorrow Teddy would be giving her her surprise present of pearls. *Two* rows of pearls which she would wear to Marion's party, together with her new woollen dress and her new hairstyle which dear Pierre had explained was based on the Empire beauties, and *no* Madame, a tumble of chestnut curls was not too young for a lady of such changeless charm!

That night, Bea wrapped her presents, including a brief-case for Ben, who was a damned nice boy and only needed a bit of guidance to be turned into a thoroughly good egg. She was particularly proud of Stephen's present, which was a silver-topped walking stick which Dorothy had found, and very cheap too! She tied on the label, which simply said: 'From the bossiest of all your *many* females!', before adding it to the rest of the parcels on her dressing table, a picture of Joss staring down at her from the wall behind.

'Hallo, old friend,' she remarked, for just lately she had taken to talking to Joss, as well as to herself and Marion's ginger cat.

'Tomorrow we'll all be together again and eating too much, and no doubt thinking of when we were eating too little. Still, life must go on, I suppose.'

And it did.

On Christmas morning, Marion's friends arrived by bus, taxi, a hired car and a sports car, disgorging themselves into a house that had miraculously straightened itself and was festive with holly and mistletoe, plus a gigantic tree covered in unwound tinsel, and candles twisted like sticks of barley sugar. And when, after tea, Marion turned out the lights and lighted the candles, the tree and the room were everything that the women had conjured up to keep themselves sane in the camps.

The room glowed in the lights from the tree and the fire, and had that particular smell which always spells Christmas: a metallic singe of tinsel, mingling with pine and a turkey that even now cooked in the oven that couldn't cook anything.

And when Blanche and her small brother dived for their presents, the past was buried under the bright wrappings that everyone, even Dominica, was tearing off and throwing across the carpet as they Ahhhed and Ooohhed at their gifts – even while they watched everyone else's reaction as their own were unwrapped.

And later, when they were wearing paper hats and sitting at a table scattered with pulled crackers and the débris of a Christmas dinner, Marion stood up and proposed the toast that she had proposed every year since the fall of Singapore.

'To absent friends.'

The heat inside the Centre was unbelievable, but then, as Kate remarked to Duncan, what can you expect when the place is jam-packed with refugees, ex-patients, friends, and anyone else who happened to have nowhere to go for Christmas.

They were laying out the buffet lunch, which had been donated by a friend who owned a restaurant, and which had arrived in a cart pulled by two of the oldest Chinese Kate had ever clapped eyes on.

'So here's to us,' she announced to Duncan, sipping a Tiger beer; but his hands were full of plates, so all he could do was to shout 'Here, here', as he staggered across the school room and dumped them on a trestle table covered in a Russian shawl donated by Madam Evansky.

Outside in the courtyard, Sister Ulrica was telling the children the story of the Nativity, and reciting a very long list of all the animals who had been in the stable, because children loved lists as much as they loved animals; and if she added a monkey and snake it was only because these were the animals they knew, and how can you understand any story unless you can put yourself in it?

'Yes, my little May, there *was* a kitten called Pudding, who was playing with the tassel which hung from the cloak of one of the three Wise Men, so will you please let me get on or we won't have time for our feast.'

Kate eased her aching back as she marvelled at the sheer stamina of Ulrica, who seemed none the worse for being shot. In fact, had informed her that the Good Lord had sent the bullet so that she might rest.

Not that she needed a rest now, thought Kate, for hadn't she arrived at dawn with her good friend Father

Joseph, who had unloaded a vast cauldron of cooked rice in case the Centre might not have enough.

'I must return immediately,' the father had told them firmly, 'or my life won't be worth tuppence, because Sister Anna needs the jeep while her own is getting a rebore.' Not that this had stopped him joining them in a drink of celebration, the wine spilling down his cassock and mingling with the various other stains that his inept hands had managed to scatter.

'So here's to us all, and may the Good Lord look down on our venture and bless it,' he declared. 'And bless this dear country, that it might soon learn the ways of peace, and in doing so heal its wounds.'

In the cell of Changi prison, Christina again examined the cards which had been sent to her from England and Singapore.

It had been kind of them to remember, considering what had happened, but oh how absurd they were: the Victorian scene of a street in an English village; the robin perched on a branch; and most of all, the picture of a naked baby and the Virgin Mary wearing a red dress edged with blue velvet and shot with gold.

She was not a Christian, but even so . . . The poor girl would have been dressed in rags, and the baby wouldn't have been plump and white, but thin and wrinkled and probably with a skin exactly the same colour as her own . . .

How odd that she had never thought of them as displaced persons before, when that was what they had been: leaving their home to pay taxes to a conqueror who had plundered their lands and crucified anyone who didn't hold the same belief as their own. And now she came to think of it, those who weren't killed outright, would have been locked in a prison, just as she was locked in a prison now.

Two thousand years of struggle, and nothing has changed, thought Christina; for the first time in her life realising that she bore the name of a religion in which she had never believed.

Wouldn't you know it, she told herself, smiling at the many ironies of her life. And when the guard unlocked the door and shouted 'Tea up and a happy Christmas' she actually thanked him without even noticing that she had done so.

But then, tea was the one thing they all had in common; which, ridiculous though it might seem, could be looked on as some kind of start . . .

Post·A·Book

A Royal Mail service in association with the Book Marketing Council & The Booksellers Association.

Post-A-Book is a Post Office trademark.